W9-APR-319

The DEAD Do Not IMPROVE

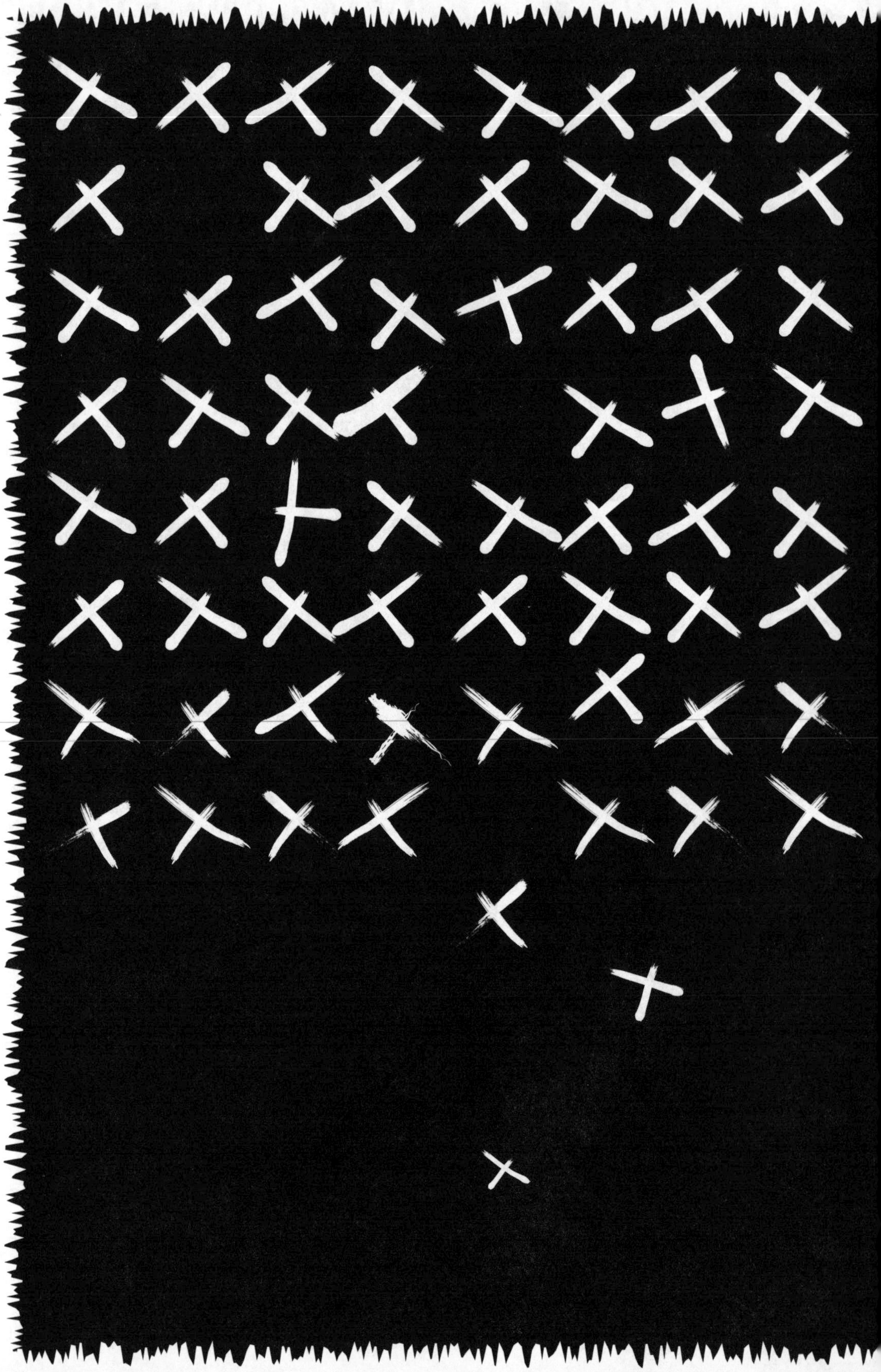

The DEAD Do Not IMPROVE

JAY CASPIAN KANG

Margaret E. Heggan Public Library
606 Delsea Drive
Sewell, NJ 08080

A NOVEL

 HOGARTH · LONDON · NEW YORK

This is a work of fiction. Names, characters, places, and incidents either are the product of the author's imagination or are used fictitiously. Any resemblance to actual persons, living or dead, events, or locales is entirely coincidental.

Copyright © 2012 by Jay Caspian Kang

All rights reserved.
Published in the United States by Hogarth, an imprint of the Crown Publishing Group, a division of Random House, Inc., New York.
www.crownpublishing.com

HOGARTH is a trademark of the Random House Group Limited, and the H colophon is a trademark of Random House, Inc.

Library of Congress Cataloging-in-Publication Data is available upon request.

ISBN 978-0-307-95388-9
eISBN 978-0-307-95390-2

Printed in the United States of America

Book design by Maria Elias
Jacket design and hand lettering by Gray318
Jacket illustration by Christopher Brand
Author photograph by Eric Wolfinger

10   9   8   7   6   5   4   3   2   1

First Edition

To my parents and my sister

†

The DEAD Do Not IMPROVE

DIAL M FOR MURDEROUSNESS

1. The Baby Molester and I talked only twice. The first time, she knocked on my door and asked for four eggs. I remember being amused by the anachronism—what sort of person still asks her neighbor for eggs?—until I realized it had been years since I'd had a single egg in my refrigerator, much less four.

The second time she knocked, it was well past midnight on some blown-out Tuesday. I was clicking through Craigslist w4m's, my head swimming in a desperate, almost haikulike fog—"oh my loneliness / it rolls through the foggy bay / here it comes. Again!" When I heard the knock, I hurried to the door, anticipating some new girl, the sort of beautiful girl who, when her hair is wet from the rain, looks more like a planet than a girl. But it was just the Baby Molester in a peach slip. And one limpening sock. The light from an earth-friendly bulb cut through that electric hair, exposing a fragile, mottled quail egg of a skull. A look somewhere close to smugness hovered over her shiny face. She asked for a cigarette and, after an awkward pause, asked for two. She had a guest, she explained. I gave her five and really considered asking her some questions, but did not.

2. It was Kathleen who came up with the name Baby Molester. This was three years ago, at a concert in Golden Gate Park. I had just moved to San Francisco from New York. Staring down at the mass of dank heads, I asked Kathleen, "Who knew an entire city could be filled with ugly white people?" She said, "Calm down. This is a bluegrass festival." On a dirt patch by the stage, this old hippie was stomping up a cloud of dust. Two young girls danced at her feet, clapping like drunken seals. A woman, hopefully the mother, hovered nearby, forcing the sort of smile that is forced more in San Francisco than anywhere else in this country.

Later, at a dustier, abandoned stage, we saw her again. This time she was dancing with someone else's little boy. His red beret stayed on his head by some miracle of centrifugal force. His chubby, inscrutable face was contorted into the look of a young child who is contemplating whether to cry—the wide-open eyes, the twittering chin designed to stop even the most militant of spinster armies. Kathleen murmured, "There are so many reasons why a woman that age would feel the need to molest other people's babies." After a pause, she added, "And each one of them is heartbreaking." I murmured my agreement, said something devastating about the failure of the sixties, and spent the rest of the night feeling superior to the entire state of California.

Two weeks later, when I moved into my own apartment, the Baby Molester was sitting on the stoop. I called Kathleen and marveled at the smallness of the city. She said, "Yeah, it's a small city. But all cities are small, you know?"

I tried to not hate her for saying something so stupid. But, you know.

3 .   I confess: I slept through the whole thing. Through the gunshots, the police sirens, the ambulance, the detective who might have knocked on my door, the hushed discussions of the neighbors. And since there was no real reason to leave the apartment the next day, I did not witness any of the police tape or the shattered glass or the crime reporters or the wary gang members walking up and down the street just to make sure.

I LEARNED ABOUT the death of the Baby Molester because I was bored and Googling myself. I had found nothing but the same shit I always find—a five-hundred-word essay I had written for a now-defunct blog about how *Illmatic* had helped me grieve for my dead parents (number 14 in search), a published excerpt of my ultimately unpublished novel (number 183 in search), a pixelated photo of me, fatter, reading at a bar in Brooklyn (number 2 in image search). I was once again humiliated to know that my version of "Philip Kim" could elicit nothing more than those three flags stuck in the landscape of all the other Philip Kims of the world. Desperate (again) to find something else, I added my address into the search with a litany of hopefully descriptive keywords: ASIAN, THIN, ATHLETIC, LONG-HAIRED, BROODING, CHEEKBONES.

My hope was that some girl might have watched me lean up against a tree or maybe light a cigarette or pet an agreeable dog or frown over a burnt cup of coffee and maybe she might have caught my eye and maybe she might have decided to post something cute and short in "Missed Encounters" or some forum like that, on the decent chance that I might, in fact, be trolling the Internet for her.

When I narrowed the search by Googling my cross-streets, a link appeared to a story in the *Chronicle*'s crime blog: WOMAN SLAIN IN MISSION DISTRICT. The details were spare—the location, the age of the victim, the adjective "elderly."

I knew it was her. Our block is short and lined with lime trees, and every other old lady I've seen walking around is Mexican.

After some deliberation, I called Kathleen. She sounded weary and practical, and although it had been over a year since we had spoken last, she politely consoled me over the murder of my neighbor, citing statistics, the fragility of our lives. One day, you take the 31 to Golden Gate Park to dance with the children of people who see you as nothing but a testament to the exhausting reality of idealism. Sometime later, an illegal immigrant fires a gun on your street, and the bullet, by force of infinitesimal chance, or God, shatters your sole window and, deflected slightly by the impact, travels exactly to the spot where you have decided to put your head for the night.

She said, "Crazier things happen all the time. You know?"

I said, "That's retarded."

She said, "What?"

"You're being retarded."

"Why do you even care so much? You told me you talked to her twice."

"Why don't you care?"

"Because it's senseless and insane to worry about stray bullets. Think of the odds."

"Well, I have to care about it. I don't have your luxury."

"What?"

"She lived next door to me."

She snorted.

A cautious distance colors us all banal. At least that's the tendency. I said someone was waiting for me and hung up the phone.

After twenty, thirty minutes on the couch, I was over it. I put on my pants and left the apartment.

4.   Outside, the only remaining evidence was a shattered windowpane and a sagging, trampled perimeter of police tape. Someone had smeared a pinkish substance on the white slatting that framed the window. Upon closer inspection, the pink stuff appeared to be lipstick.

Across the street, a young couple stared woefully at the crime scene. They lived in one of the gentrifier condos. The guy was always making an effort to talk to the block's indigenous Mexicans. In two years, neither the guy nor the girl had ever said a word to me because their safety was not compromised by my presence. The girl was the sort of girl who looks best in jeans and a performance fleece. She had an extraordinary ass. The man owned, but rarely rode, a turquoise Vespa.

When he saw me walking down the steps to the sidewalk, the guy shrugged, but with meaning. Because I am a bit of a coward, I shook my head, approximating his meaning. My way of saying, "It's a damn shame." To those people.

5. I wandered around for a while before admitting there was nowhere to go, so I ducked into BEAN and took a seat near the bathrooms. I hated everything about BEAN—the unfinished ceilings, the Eames-wonderful chairs, the sanitary tables, the architectural cappuccinos, the barrel-aged indie rock. Still, I was always finding myself there, partly because it was a half block from my apartment, but also because I, demographic slave, am always finding myself in the places I hate the most.

I ordered a cappuccino and read the *Chronicle*'s crime section. Someone got beaten badly on 26th and Treat. A pizza shop was held up in Oakland. Under a footbridge in the Tenderloin, police found a homeless man who had been stabbed to death. My mind drifted to some detective story I had read back in college, and although I could recall the author's name and the particulars of the story, I could not translate what any of it was supposed to mean. I did remember that the corpse in the story was not a corpse until it became a corpse again. And that at the end, through some trick of logic, which might or might not have been inspired by Schrödinger's cat, it turned out the corpse had never been a corpse at all. I remembered not really understanding anything, really, but I did remember a girl in the class who everyone called Pooch Cooch, and remembered Pooch Box wore white and pearl earrings, and remembered that I, absurdly, had felt sorry for her. And finally, I remembered that my confusion over the story had, in part, helped convince me to give up my scholarly ambitions.

As I was sitting in BEAN, amid the city's aesthetically unemployed, the memory of my stupidity still embarrassed me. Since college, I had read maybe two hundred, three hundred books and even tried my hand at writing a difficult novel. Did it not stand to reason, then, that I might have somehow, unknowingly, developed the skills to understand the meaning of the corpse? I really considered walking up the street to the used bookstore to have a crack at redemption, but I had spent two hours in there a few days back. The girl behind the counter had a perfectly symmetrical haircut and stared impassively at everyone who entered the store. Her recommendation shelf floated nicely between the listless ether of Joan Didion's female narrators and the histories of hardscrabble things: car bombs, prison gangs, crystal meth. How could I face her twice in a week?

I sat in my seat instead. Read the paper, jotted pretend notes to myself on a napkin. One read: "WILLIE MCGEE." Another read: "You say, I talk slow all the time." A couple hours passed like that. By the time Adam walked into BEAN, I had completely forgotten about the Baby Molester.

6. Adam was from my time in New York. We both entered Columbia's graduate creative writing program at the age of twenty-three. Neither of us really ever had anything to write about, but we held to the credo that all young, privileged men in their twenties should never ever discuss their lives in any meaningful way. Our stories were about boredom, porn, child geniuses, talking dogs.

We spent three, four years that way, telling the same jokes. Adam eventually picked up a variety of drug habits because he thought they would provide a grittier spin on the traditional American Jewish experience. They did not. As for me, all my morose, nameless narrators had two living parents, and, although people were always dying, nobody ever succumbed to stomach cancer or a car wreck. To all those raceless men, death was funny or it was strange, but it was never talked about, at least not directly.

When it became clear that the thriftily coiffed girls of the publishing industry were just not that into me, I moved to San Francisco to follow Kathleen. Adam had just started dating a hard-luck porn star in North Hollywood. A year and a half later, he showed up in San Francisco with his father's car and a new girlfriend.

At some point, it became clear we had to find work. Adam started teaching creative writing at a school for the criminally insane. I got a job editing content for a website providing emotional help for men recently abandoned by loved ones.

7. Adam sat down at my table without a word of welcome. It could no longer count as coincidence, us finding each other here. We talked about TV, fantasy football, breasts. Outside, the fog had condensed down to a drizzle. The baristas started up their chatter. One was worried the rain would drive the crackheads underneath the awnings, meaning she would have to perfectly time her trip to the bus stop. Another said she liked the rain because it reminded her of her favorite soul song. Adam took a bad novel out of his jacket and began to read. I took my laptop out of my bag and read through my dumb e-mail. After a while, Adam asked, "What's good?"

"Good?"

"Good."

"Odd word choice."

"Why?"

I pointed at the computer screen. "What could be good?"

"You on Craigslist?"

"No."

"Well, that's your problem. On Craigslist, things can be good."

The mention of Craigslist loosed a current of shame. I thought about the grainy, dimly lit women of the previous night—the camera angles that soften noses, the anonymous, truncated breasts, the loose attempts at dignity, the unabashed anatomy, the ball-crushing loneliness, the labyrinthine possibilities of hyperlinks; all of it reminded me that my neighbor had been murdered the night before.

I told Adam about it. He arched his eyebrows and asked, "Through the window, just like that, huh?"

"Yeah. I don't think it was a stray bullet, though. Somebody had taken the time to smear some pink shit all around the window."

"Fucking biblical, man."

"It wasn't blood."

"You said it was pink?"

"Like lipsticky pink."

Adam stuck his pinkie in his coffee and frowned. He said, "Easy explanation. Gang violence. Nortenos. That's their color."

"She was like a sixty-year-old white woman."

"Exactly. They want los gringos like us out of their neighborhoods."

"I feel it necessary to remind you that I'm not white."

"Did you read *Mission Dishin'* this morning?"

"Yeah."

"Some dude got beat up. A tech nerd."

"I saw that."

"Up on Treat."

"I saw it."

"That's like eight dudes getting beat this month. And then your neighbor gets shot. You don't think there's something going on?"

I confess it made me feel a little important.

8.　　Adam went back to reading his book. An e-mail from my boss arrived in my inbox:

FROM: bill <bill@getoverit.com>

TO: phil <phil@getoverit.com>

phil. here are today's gold members. get back to me.

A spreadsheet was attached. Twenty-six names in all.

The company had recently put a significant amount of money into targeted advertising, a departure from the previous strategy of placing banner ads on any porn sites offering free trailers. The old idea was that men who had recently broken up with their girlfriends would probably increase their porn intake, but not to the point where they would be willing to hand over a credit card number.

It was stupid, but it wasn't my idea. The porn trailer idea resulted in the worst quarter in the company's three-year history. Meetings were called. Surveys were passed around to the employees. In the end, some genius who wasn't me figured out that if you could somehow probe a person's e-mail for certain keyword combinations—broken + heart, never + felt + so + lonely, dumped + me/her, ended + things, destined + to + end, what + happened, fucking + bullshit, slut + bag—you could more accurately narrow down your customer base. Contracts were signed with all the prominent social networking sites and every major e-mail provider. Within the first three months, the site saw a 550 percent jump in hits and a 300 percent jump in subscriptions. We expanded our services.

My job was to send out a personalized e-mail to each of the new clients, congratulating them for taking this courageous and worthwhile step forward.

9.

FROM: phil <phil@getoverit.com>
TO: Richard McBeef <rmcbeef22@yahoo.com>

Hey Richard,

This is Phil from getoverit.com, your Personal Break-Up Coach. Just wanted to introduce myself and let you know how excited I am to start working with you. My buddy from college works in IT, so I understand the stress and pressures of the profession. Like you, this buddy of mine had a girlfriend who couldn't handle his success and ended up sleeping with some absolute loser. Let's talk about it. Whenever you're comfortable.

Phil Davis

FROM: phil <phil@getoverit.com>

TO: Tom Nichols <tdnichols@imagineengines.com>

Hey Tom,

This is Phil from getoverit.com, your Personal Break-Up Coach. Just wanted to introduce myself and let you know how excited I am to start working with you. My buddy from college works in engineering, so I understand the stress and pressures of the profession. Like you, this buddy of mine had a girlfriend who couldn't handle his success and ended up sleeping with some absolute loser. Let's talk about it, bro. Whenever you're comfortable.

Phil Davis

"How do you do it?" Adam was reading over my shoulder.

"Control-C, Control-V."

"That's awful, man."

"You'd get used to it."

"They make you sign with your slave master's name?"

"Nobody trusts an Oriental with love advice."

"Control-C, Control-V, indeed."

"Hey, did you send this e-mail as a joke?"

"What? No."

"Check out this name."

"Richard McBeef?"

"I assumed it was you."

"Nope. Are you hungry?"

I pointed at the flaky remains of my croissant.

"Pastries don't count. Too much air."

"I guess."

"Okay. Nachos, then."

10.   We walked onto Valencia Street into the grayness of another foggy morning. In places like San Francisco that are choked by fog, even the bluest, clearest day always carries a tinge of remembered gray. So this housing project, painted canary and cardinal red, surrounded on all sidewalks by plots of pioneer flowers, still pulses grayly up Valencia to 16th, where the anonymous buildings are all hotels like the Sunshine Hotel or the Hotel 16 or the Hotel Mission or the Hotel Ignacio or even the Hotel St. Francis, where the sign in the window reads, "WE NO LONGER RENT ROOMS BY THE HOUR," a hopeful declaration, somehow. When I voted for Obama, I stood in line with a man from the Hotel St. Francis who looked exactly like Cornel West, but insane and with bits of powdered doughnut stuck in his beard. He asked me if this was the polling station for the Hotel St. Francis, and when I shrugged, he said he was being disenfranchised because you can live in the Hotel St. Francis for years—the man at the front desk will know when you've gone on your run, the girl who is too young to live in the Hotel St. Francis will fall in love and buy you a pair of socks—but you certainly cannot have a voter registration card delivered there. During a childhood road trip to the Blue Ridge Mountains, my father explained the difference between hotels and motels. Hotels, he said, are more expensive. Now I know he was wrong. Hotels are just motels, but romanticized somehow. These collapsing

Margaret E. Heggan Public Library
606 Delsea Drive
Sewell, NJ 08080

buildings are hotels to the people who keep *L'Étranger* and *Howl* stashed under their pillows, who try heroin once before realizing they only like the literary strain of the drug, who see a bit of crazy wisdom in the shit-stained, misspelled cardboard signs of the homeless, who stand in front of the Hotel St. Francis and look in through the smoggy picture window at the backboard, where forty-two actual keys dangle the same way they might have dangled in a more humane time. Beyond the front desk, the lobby opens up, green as a Barnes & Noble bathroom. Twenty or so plastic Adirondacks are clustered in hostile little arrangements, each one angled at a five-hundred-pound television. A chandelier, dusty, incomplete, provides a rebuttal to the fluorescent stringers overhead, a soft, nearly sepia rebuttal, which, on more than one occasion, lulled up the slouching figures of Arturo Bandini, Steve Earle, Fuckhead, Jim Stark, Knut Hamsun, and Ronizm in those Adirondack chairs. But then, invariably, the fluorescent stringers will flicker or one of the tenants will stand up or a dead smell will gather and my old favorite literary losers will turn back into the crackheads of the Mission who are all defeated in the same way.

Still. I admit it. There were times when I stood in front of the window of the Hotel St. Francis, stared in at the squalor, thick and silent as an oil spill, and wished my prospects had shaded a bit blacker.

II. In the rust-girded doorway to the Taqueria Cancun, five kids in oversized white T-shirts huddled around two lit cigarettes. Last week, *Mission Dishin'*, a neighborhood events blog targeted at the seventh wave of gentrifiers, had broken the story that these Latino kids in oversized white T-shirts were, in fact, gangsters.

Adam and I belonged to an earlier generation of hipster/gentrifier dinosaurs and were therefore too old to take *Mission Dishin'* seriously. Meaning, even though neither of us really liked the Taqueria Cancun, and even though both of us were scared of the Mara Salvatruchas, we had to keep going there.

There is no logic to this, sure. But I keep doing shit for these exact reasons.

We pushed past the kids without incident.

After retrieving our nachos and beer, we sat down at the end of a heavily lacquered picnic table. I asked Adam, "What do you want to do later?"

"Don't know. Probably stay in."

"Are you still watching that Ronizm video?"

"It's research."

"Have you figured anything out?"

"These are terrible."

"I told you we should've gone up the street. They use fucked-up cheese here. It's, like, Swiss or something."

"Up the street is five blocks away."

"I meant about the video. If you've figured anything out."

We kept picking at the nachos until they devolved into a block of congealed cheese, soggy chip shards, dehydrating, graying beans. Every twenty minutes on the dot, the neon jukebox would light up on its own, announcing, with a fanfare of horns, accordions, the start of yet another sad ranchera song, which, although I, sad dinosaur, would never admit it, sounded just like every other sad ranchera song.

A threesome of girls in glasses sat down at the other end of the picnic table and asked us some questions about the neighborhood. We both muttered something about the Phone Booth and got up to leave. There is no pretty way to finish off a plate of nachos. Our beers were gone.

Outside, the five kids in the doorway had become nine, the two cigarettes a stubby four. Something, a furtive look, a slight swing of the shoulder, must have given us away. The spaces between the bodies squeezed tighter. Just as I was prepping my best-learned reaction, the shoulders parted and let me pass. I looked back. Through a hedgerow of bushy black ponytails, Adam's face blanked out into a practiced hey-we're-cool smile.

The tallest of the kids stepped directly into Adam's path and asked, "Dude, what are you doing here?"

Adam, deflating, said, "Hey, David, how's the story going?"

"Not bad, man. What you getting, some food?"

"Yeah, food."

"Burrito?"

"No."

"Tacos?"

"No."

"Nachos?"

"Yes."

I understood his shame. It was a bit embarrassing to admit to these kids, or anyone, really, that you were eating nachos. Again, I felt the shitty lack of my own minority status. Despite my most silent, most earnest wishes, people were never embarrassed to tell me about their latest adventures with kimchi.

"They're terrible here."

"I know."

"If you knew, why didn't you just go to Farolito? Too far away?"

"Yeah."

The kid cocked his head back in my direction. He asked, "Adam, who's that?"

It occurred to me that I should act as naturally as possible. With hands spread at my sides, I craned my head up toward the sky and announced, "It's still raining."

"Yo, Adam, you gay?"

"Why?"

"Who is that?"

"My friend. From New York City."

"His pants are tight as fuck, man."

It was true. I worried, of course, about my bulge.

"We gotta get going, David. But I'll see you in class on Monday, right?"

"Of course. I got some more fucked-up shit for you, Adam."

The huddle parted. Adam came out smiling, nodding. We walked away. When we were a good two blocks away, I asked, "One of your students?"

"Advanced creative writing."

"Advanced? Is he good?"

"Really fucked-up shit. Like lions with guns, lots of dead hookers."

"That doesn't sound too bad."

"It's not."

"He called you by your first name."

"Where are you living, man?"

12. We ended up at Adam's apartment. A menorah, mottled, oxidized green, stood in the only window. Cigarette butts had long since replaced the candles. There was a futon, I guess. A sparkling flat-panel television provided the apartment's only light—an interring blue that lacquered the scarred bamboo floors, the checkerboard linoleum of the kitchenette, the brass of the menorah, the matte of Adam's guitar cases and amps, even the blue-orange coat of Geronimo Rex, Adam's morbidly obese cat, which greeted our entry with an upraised paw.

It was a horrible place. But it had that big TV, so it was better than my place.

Adam put on the video.

THREE MONTHS AGO, as a gesture of reparation to the rappers she had condemned in years past, Oprah aired a special on Ronizm, a Queensbridge emcee who blew up in 1993 when his debut album, *All the Words Past the Margin,* went generational. Adam and I were both twelve when *All the Words* dropped, too young to bump it in our mother's car but just old enough to recall our first encounters with it, the way an adult, recently bruised, might suddenly remember a childhood sledding accident.

To middling applause, Ronizm was wheeled out onto Oprah's stage by DJ Speck. Old clothes on old sticks, Ronizm's trademark denim coat hung badly off his shoulders, his Wayfarers dangled awkwardly off the tip of a collapsing nose. Although they tried, the blacked-out lenses couldn't quite obscure the ruins of big chief cheekbones sunk into their own hollows.

When the applause puttered out, Oprah said hello. Then she asked Ronizm something about his childhood.

In his gravelly monotone, Ronizm said, "My pops was this alto saxo-phonist from Queens and my mom raised me and my sister there, but my pops was always all over the place—Manhattan, Jersey, Philly, the Chi, LA, Mobile, wherever his next gig was at, but when he was home, he would introduce me to all the coolest cats up in Queensbridge."

Oprah interrupted to ask something. Ronizm continued: "You know, even now, when I listen to the songs off my first two albums, I realize the pushers, players, pimps, and whatnot in the songs aren't the cats from back in my day, but actually they're the pushers, players, and pimps from way back in the day, when my pops was young, like back in '69, '72, back right when I was just being born."

Oprah asked a follow-up question, but before Ronizm could answer, I wrestled the remote control away from Adam and hit fast forward.

"What are you doing? It was getting good."

"Who can watch this shit?"

"Just watch him do the song."

We watched in 4× speed for a bit. When Oprah finally cleared the stage, I hit play. Ronizm, feet dangling off the edge of a high chair, mic clasped in hands, bopped his head to Strictly Legal's opening instrumen-tal: the loose snare, the Primo scratches, the wandering horn. (Once, while on ecstasy in college, I sat down naked at my computer, put on Strictly Legal, and wrote 4,200 words on why, if I were to die and be re-incarnated as a deaf man, my only phantom sounds would be the perfect rattle of these opening bars.) But while the twin miracles of recording technology and nostalgia kept the track pristine, Ronizm, himself, was mostly gone. His voice was bombed out. What was once heraldic, hard, weatherproof, was now a spume, sputtering and depleted.

It's a weird hurt, isn't it, to watch a dying rapper? Ronizm, my number three emcee of all time, following Nas and Big L, had become a gushy old man, talking, like all gushy old men, about the good old days, the good old days.

13. After my mother died of stomach cancer in 1995, two months short of my sixteenth birthday, my father, clumsy bear, did his best to corral us into a renewed paradigm of fatherhood. It was an admirable resolution, sure, but one without a target audience. There wasn't much wrong with my sister, so he just kind of checked over her homework and monitored her always-modest hemlines. My own algorithm of GPA (4.67 weighted), test scores (1,480 SAT), athletic achievement (two years of JV baseball), extracurricular activity (two-time North Carolina policy debate champion), and socialization (virginity lost in 1994 to Ruth Stein), while not optimal, wasn't bad enough to warrant attention. My assorted troubles (two suspensions for mouthing off to teachers, five reported fights, two wins over Amos Mays, two clear losses to Daunte Degraffenreid, one inconclusive with Javon Jeffries, marijuana possession, general surliness) fit in somewhere in his conception of an appropriate youth.

Hungry bear, my father, he rooted around until he found something. Try to understand, his brother lost his liquor store in the Rodney King riots. When my father heard the news, he grabbed a wrench and banged out a dent in the pole that held up my basketball hoop. Who knows if he intended the troubling symbolism, but there it was. And so, three years later, when he witnessed his only son accumulate a very specific set of affectations—the slurring of mannered syllables, a darkening of denims, Clark Wallabees with disastrous dye jobs (candy apple red and the blue ones on the Ghostface album cover), camo hoodies, Maxwell tapes wrapped in poorly photocopied images of project buildings, a copy of *Soul on Ice* (never read), a legal pad filled with doodles of imagined teks and snippets of my very own battle punch lines (mostly involving rhyming "mental" with "Oriental")—how could he have not seen my slow, accessorized descent into blackness as his great cause?

Toothless bear now, the slowness of my mother's death had sapped out his meanness. Instead of simply beating the hip-hop out of me, he took me to a Bob Dylan concert up in Richmond. He let me drive. I can still remember the trees along the 85 and how each one looked the same, cut in a straight line, and how my father, at ease in the passenger's seat, had his small hands folded on his flat stomach. When the endlessness of Virginia became intolerable, he told me about how he and my mother would order takeout black bean noodles to their apartment in Seoul and crouch over the radio in their cramped, grimy kitchen. Every Wednesday at 6 P.M., their friend had a show on their college's station. He played anything in English but always ended the show with his favorite Bob Dylan song: "I'm a Believer."

I didn't correct him, but the damage was done. I pictured my father and my mother sharing a bowl of noodles in their apartment in Seoul. In the photos they have from that time, even poor lighting and communist film cannot hide the cracked paint on the walls, my mother's incandescent beauty. A small radio is playing the Monkees, and my parents, equipped with two years of college English, are feverishly trying to decipher the revolutionary message in "I'm a Believer":

"I'm in rub. Now I a be-ree-vah. I a be-ree-vah, I couldn't reave her if I try."

THE CROWD THAT day was a chorus of satisfied exhales. We found a spot on a hillside, just a stone's throw from a historical preservation placard, but neither of us could quite make out the text. I said it was probably something about the Civil War. The crowd filled in, the air thickened. My father, starving bear, shrank in the grass and disappeared.

On the drive back, he leaned up against the door with his eyes shut and toggled the power locks in time with the music from the oldies station. When we began to drift out of range, he asked if I had brought any of my rap tapes along. I only had *The Shogun's Decapitator*. When it was over, we grabbed a snack at a Bojangles drive-through near the Virginia–North Carolina border. Mouth full of chicken, he pointed at the tape deck and said, "I can't understand ninety percent what he say. Can you understand?"

YEARS LATER, I told my history of jazz professor about this trip with my father to go see Dylan. I think I used the word "overrated." He shook his head and said that I would never understand because I hadn't been around to witness *Blonde on Blonde*, at least not in its proper context. As for my father, he said, "It's hard to imagine how someone who didn't live in America at the time could really *feel* Dylan, because, as you know, so much of Dylan is about the history, of course, within its proper musical context."

That was the first time I've ever really considered killing somebody. I really considered cracking his skull open with some funny object—a saxophone, a dildo, maybe.

Something awful, dark, must have flashed across my face. He asked what was wrong.

I CAN STILL feel that violence within me, but its pathways have become more twisted, serpentine, and, ultimately, inert. At least once a week, I'll weigh the option of hurting someone. There's never any pattern, or specificity, really.

I used to think I could turn that violence into fiction—this idea was inspired, more than I'd like to admit, by Eminem—but fiction requires a steadier logic of who and why, good and bad, absurd and real. Violence, even when it's supposed to be chaotic, is never truly chaotic. Poe's ourang-outang, who rips apart the women of the Rue Morgue and stuffs them up in the chimney, is studied as the solution to a puzzle, or, misguidedly, as a racist allegory. What he is not, however, is simply a lustful orangutan who got away and killed some women. He is not a symbol of insanity.

Were I a better writer, I'd make myself into that symbol.

14.　Adam nodded off on the couch. It was four in the afternoon. I let myself out and walked back home. At the end of my block, I stood in front of the Laundromat's exhaust and stared out at the lime trees as a whorl of fuzzy-smelling steam swirled around my feet. I thought, "This is a Stygian scene," and then thought about the movie *Taxi Driver*, and then *Meet the Parents*. Despite my efforts, the steam and the fog rolling down from Noe Valley, the visions of Travis Bickle, and the repetition in my head of the words "The Baby Molester is dead," all those signifying things couldn't convince me that hell lay ahead. Instead, I wondered about my e-mail.

Up the block, a blond head popped out of a gentrifier window. It was Performance Fleece. She was staring down at a sky blue Astro van double-parked outside my building. I didn't want to make eye contact, so I took out my cell phone and started hitting random buttons. The word I spelled, incidentally, was "FLAMER." I would've kept texting all the way to my front door, but as I passed the gentrifier condo's graffiti-proof metal door, something splattered on the sidewalk next to me.

It was a yogurt cup.

I looked up. Performance Fleece jerked her head in the direction of the van.

I wasn't getting it. I worried my gigantic head would look even bigger from three stories up. Does distance, with its inexhaustible cache of favors, extend the same grace to us bobbleheads that it extends to the tanned, snaggle-faced gym addicts of San Diego?

Something behind me buzzed. It occurred to me that professional basketball players, when viewed from the upper deck of an arena, always look like normal-size people. So, given that my head was approximately the size of a basketball, a woman's basketball, it stood to reason . . .

A second yogurt cup hit the sidewalk, this time accompanied by a plastic spoon. Performance Fleece's head reappeared in the window. She looked disappointed in me. Not knowing what to do, I pointed at the yogurt cup and smiled. She shook her head in disbelief and mouthed something. From where I was standing, it looked like, "The gay, the gay," but, after a flurry of angry pointing, it became clear that what she meant was, "The gate, the gate."

I nodded. She ducked away. The buzzing started up again. It was, indeed, the condo's front gate. I pushed my way inside.

The lobby was clean. That's all I can really say about it. I did note a Paisley settee, but only because I had just learned the week before what a settee was. A loud thudding came from the staircase, and when it finally stopped, Performance Fleece sprang into view. It hurt, at least little a bit, to hear her clunk around in such a plebeian way.

With a withering, who-farted look on her face, she motioned me up the stairs. I followed her great ass up two flights and through a heavy door and into a condo that also doesn't really need to be described.

Then (Hallelujah!), with all of Deerfield Academy behind her voice, she asked, "Are you retarded?"

"What's up?"

She pointed out the window and said, "That van hasn't moved for two hours now."

I failed to see the problem. There were always cars double-parked on our block. I shrugged. Performance Fleece pointed a long, thin finger at my nose. I caught a whiff of cocoa butter. My mounting erection was confused by this. She asked, "Are you high? Mel says you always look high."

"Mel?"

"My fucking boyfriend. You met him this morning."

Women of America! Take note: Learn to say "fuck" and "boyfriend" with the same even mix of contempt and protectiveness and you will never be lonely again.

"Oh, he didn't tell me his name."

"That van hasn't moved in two hours. About an hour ago, a kid got out and kind of kicked around in the dirt in front of your building."

"Maybe he lost something?"

"Of course he lost something. He lost his bullets in that poor old lady's face."

"Oh, I see."

"Yes."

"Well, why would he come back to the scene of the crime? Wouldn't he be in El Salvador by now?"

"Did you see the red paint smeared around the window? That's a gang sign."

My reason was returning to me. I asked, "Okay, okay. Can we think this through? Together?"

"You have to go down there."

"What?"

"To establish a strong neighborhood presence."

"Strong neighborhood presence?"

"Yes. Strong neighborhood presence."

"Well, where's Mel? Isn't that his scooter parked on the sidewalk?"

"He takes the shuttle to work."

"So, that's like a weekend scooter?"

"Why are you talking about his fucking scooter?"

"Sorry, I guess I'm trying to say."

"Yes?"

"Shouldn't we both go down there?"

She turned around and bent over to open a drawer. My God, her ass! When my eyes found their way back up to her face, she was holding a fancy kitchen knife. I worried that she might have caught me staring, but then why would she have gone for the knife before the staring had even happened? Had she been looking for something else in the drawer and, during her search, felt my eyes on her ass, and, after the moment of violation passed, chosen the knife?

I asked, "What's the knife for?"

She said, "I'm going down there with you."

15. This was Performance Fleece's plan. We would walk up and down the street, shoving our strong neighborhood presence down the throat of these gangsters.

It wasn't the most complicated plan, but what grit from Performance Fleece! What determination! What poor freshman, on which field, at which New England factory of private education and goodwill, had dared to face down this dervish? Unstoppable force, Performance Fleece, running straight toward the goal.

We took our first lap of the street. My erection felt like it was going to tear through my pants leg. But how to adjust? The waistband tuck would be too obvious. And my pants, as the advanced creative writer had pointed out, were cockblasters. By way of nervous reflex, I asked, "Where did you go to college?"

She said, "This is not the time."

"Sorry."

She grabbed my hand but did not turn to look at me. Then, with flourishing modesty, she said, "Williams."

"I went to Bowdoin."

"That's a great school."

And then we were past the van.

We walked up and down the block three more times. At each pass of the van, I made sure to ask some stupid question. Perfomance Fleece's hand was cold and well lotioned, but her palms were covered with calluses. She talked about Williams, her opinions of California, most of which had to do with political things that were foreign to me.

I talked mostly about small restaurants and small magazines. In response, she just kind of pursed her lips, asked me unrelated questions about who I knew at Bowdoin. It turned out we knew two people in common, but I only knew their names and not their faces. I took a risk and talked some shit about those two faceless people, and Performance Fleece laughed and agreed. Quickly, I forgot why we were walking or what we were doing out on the street. Girls just have that effect on me, I guess. On the fourth pass, without thinking much about it, I stared into the van.

It was the Advanced Creative Writer. He was crying into his hands. An older man with a Pancho Villa mustache was sitting in the driver's seat. He was talking to the Advanced Creative Writer, but when he caught me staring, he shut up. The Advanced Creative Writer looked up.

Then, to my horror, his eyes narrowed in recognition.

16. Both men stepped out of the car, screaming about something. I caught a couple curse words—*puta, pinche*—but everything the Advanced Creative Writer said in English was lost on me. Performance Fleece blanched and stepped away. The Advanced Creative Writer took a giant step up onto the sidewalk and pressed his scowling face up to my own.

Try to understand. I spent most of my childhood split between a foreign model of grace and my father's personal brand of macho. (I apologize for talking about him so much, but we must try to understand one another, and since we've all moved past the era when understanding was only a collection of Buddhas, zenny poems, fucking Tigers, weird pickles, and creative spins on rice, we are only left with fathers. Anyway.) After one of my fights in the middle school cafeteria with Daunte Degraffenreid, my father was called to take me home. When he walked into the office and saw me sitting on a bench next to Daunte, who, even back then, would have been described by even the most well intentioned of my friends as a "big black dude," an unrecognizable look spread across my father's face. Again, as with all of his looks, I cannot define this face as one thing or another, but with the benefit of the years (dead parents are easier to understand) and some photos of him at my sister's high school graduation, I can say that the look on his face was something akin to pride. A few years later, when I listened to Ronizm rap about how some people have to scrap to maintain dignity that is not their birthright, my thoughts on the matter were confirmed and committed to instinct. Yes, there is something about the deference of white guilt and I have certainly had my flings with it, but in the end, I've always come back to this unspoken lesson from my father: Indulge in all the liberal politics you need, son, but when it comes time to fight, you don't have the luxury to not fight.

Which is all a way of saying I slapped the shit out of the Advanced Creative Writer. It felt good. Of course it did. The man with the Pancho Villa mustache got out of the car, cursed at me, and collected the Advanced Creative Writer up off the sidewalk. As they staggered back to the van, the Advanced Creative Writer yelled, "You're fucking dead. You and your fucking girlfriend."

I looked over at Performance Fleece. Was she impressed? Had she heard the Advanced Creative Writer refer to her as my girlfriend? Ah, yes! She was chewing her lip, staring off at Mel's faggy scooter, calculating a new possibility.

17.   Performance Fleece called the police, but the dispatcher couldn't figure out how the confrontation had been the Advanced Creative Writer's fault. She suggested we try apologizing. I called Adam, but he didn't pick up. While we waited for some idea to present itself, Performance Fleece and I passed around a bottle of Macallan and watched *Access Hollywood*. Performance Fleece told me that she never liked Jennifer Aniston. Through the drinks and the *Access Hollywood*, we put together the following plausible scenario: The Advanced Creative Writer, who clearly was involved in a gang, must have accidentally shot the Baby Molester during a turf war. Racked with remorse, the Advanced Creative Writer, who, despite his gang affiliation, was a sensitive soul (hence his enrollment in advanced creative writing), confessed the crime to his father, who promptly packed his son in the family van and drove to the scene of the crime to snatch up any evidence that might criminally implicate his son. After sweeping through the dirt for bullet casings, footprints, the father had forced his son to stare in at the destroyed window, the slackening police tape that still hung across the front of the building. At this point, the Advanced Creative Writer, sensitive soul, broke down in tears.

At each commercial break, one of us would sneak up to the window to see if the van had moved. It did not move until after *Jeopardy*. By then,

Performance Fleece and I had already fucked twice. Her ass, I remember, was a bit of a disappointment, a trick of restrictive panties and $250 jeans, but she fucked like a real athlete with enthusiasm, impressive force, and limited grace.

I LEFT AT the end of a rerun of *America's Funniest Home Videos* because Mel had called to say he was finally heading back. Performance Fleece suggested that I sleep at Adam's house and copied down two phone numbers on the back of a receipt. The first was her number. The second was the number of the detective who had come by the day after the shooting. She said, "His last name is Kim, just like you, not that it means anything."

If I got in trouble, she said, call both numbers.

BOOK ONE

N o b o d y who worked in the downtown station could quite remember if Siddhartha "Sid" Finch had picked up the nickname Keanu because he had always been a surfing detective or if the nickname had been the impetus for Sid's surfing habit. Those who argued for the latter pointed to Sid's narrow face, his ethnically ambiguous eyes, which seemed half-Asian, but, in fact, were of Welsh origins, his flat, bored manner of speech. Even if Finch had never picked up a surfboard, they argued, even if Keanu Reeves's filmography had gone from the short-lived television version of *Bill and Ted's Excellent Adventure* straight to *Bill and Ted's Bogus Journey*, skipping over his only really good role as FBI agent Johnny Utah, Sid Finch would still make for a good Keanu.

Finch, as a rule, maintained that he could barely remember which version was true, and when recruits or witnesses or reporters or women asked him about the origins of his nickname, he would say, "Keanu is my middle name."

But if the inquirer was someone he instinctively liked (Finch, like all cops, only really liked people out of instinct), he would tell him the truth. Back when Finch was in the academy, a red-faced, liverous tub of guts, whose oddly tapered haircut and saggy man-tits had earned him the nickname Sergeant Bulldyke, had found Finch's slow talking so infuriating that he took to calling him Bill and Ted. The nickname led to great confusion in the classroom, especially to fellow recruits Bill Day and Ted Terpstra, who could never figure out why they were being berated in tandem. Eventually, Sergeant Bulldyke came up with Keanu as a replacement, and the name stuck.

When *Point Break* was released, Sid Finch had been Keanu for six months. It came as a great relief to Finch, who now had a better, more graceful model to pin his nickname upon. He began surfing shortly after that. As for his unusual first name, Finch's explanation was more direct. "My mother," he would say, "is a fucking hippie."

SURFING WAS WHAT was on Finch's mind as he stared down at the last known living photograph of Dolores Stone. Taken by a *Chronicle* photographer at last year's Hardly Strictly Bluegrass Festival in Golden Gate Park, it showed an old woman swinging around an unidentified child. The caption read, "Dolores Stone of San Francisco braves the chilly weather and fog at this year's Hardly Strictly Bluegrass Festival."

A half hour before, Finch had written the word "barefoot" in his notebook. He had not moved since. When Jim Kim, his phlegmatic, pockmarked partner, came barging into their shared office asking if he could borrow fifty cents, Finch managed to nod toward the dish on his desk where he kept his change. Kim grunted, stubbed his fat fingers around until he came up with two quarters, and stalked off in the general direction of the vending machines. A mild distaste settled over Finch. Kim had picked through dozens of nickels and dimes, all of which would have worked perfectly well in the station's vending machine. When Kim came back, Diet Coke in hand, Finch said something about it.

"Why would you skip over all these nickels and dimes and take two quarters?"

"What's the difference?"

"Now I have to count out five dimes the next time I go to the vending machine."

"Jesus fuck, man."

"That's how I feel."

"You take a look at those photos yet?"

Finch handed the stack of photos over to Kim, who shuffled through them quickly.

"Is that lipstick?"

"Yeah."

"Nice choice of color, especially for that neighborhood. I can't imagine the neighbors were too happy to see red on the block."

"Probably not."

"Have you looked into the seedy life of our victim yet?"

"You don't want to see those photos."

"I don't know, man. I've gotten into some weird shit in my day. Give me a hint."

"Apparently, there isn't a part of the female anatomy that doesn't wrinkle."

Kim tossed the crime scene photos back onto Finch's desk and sat down on the office's beat-up leather couch. He said, "We should be getting free sodas, anyway. My cousin works at some stupid Internet start-up a few blocks from here. They have Ping-Pong tables, TVs, and free sodas. The kid's fucking twenty-four and he's playing Ping-Pong and drinking free sodas, and here I am risking my life to pay half a dollar."

"Fifty cents is a discount."

"You should see what my mom charges at her restaurant."

"How much?"

"Two twenty-five. Can you believe that shit? The woman is an animal."

"Koreans truly are the Jews of the Orient."

"That's right. Although I should point out that you just got all fucked up 'cause I improperly borrowed your pocket change."

"That's different. It's a hygiene issue."

"Hygiene, Keanu? Do you have any idea what gets washed out onto the beaches here?"

"What were we talking about?"

"We were talking about Jews, man. Koreans as the new Jews. When white people have to stop feeling guilty about you and start planning around you, it means you've arrived. It's like that thing I was telling you about with the landlords."

"What?"

"What do you mean, what? I was telling you about it like a couple weeks ago."

"Sorry."

"It hurts me when you do this."

"Sorry."

"You really don't remember?"

"I was probably pretending to listen."

"Last year, I go to New York to visit my cousin there and I pick up a paper on the subway and there's this list of the ten worst landlords in New York City and I go down the list and it's Shlomo Rubenstein and Jew Jewbergstein and then I get to number seven, which is some Korean guy who I can't remember, like Kim Chee fucking Guevara and it's not only him, number nine is another Korean guy. I'm sitting there on the subway reading those names over and over and I feel like crying 'cause it's so beautiful. Eight Jew names and two Koreans."

"I do remember you talking about this now. But it was like six months ago."

"I'm getting choked up now just thinking about it. The media in New York needs to put Koreans on the same lists as Jews. The media doesn't give a shit about blacks and Mexicans except when they're running for president or illegally mowing some senator's lawn. But when it comes to posting some terrifying shit—like landlords who let their tenants die over fifty bucks in repairs—and it comes to naming names, then they're all over Koreans and the Jews. It's a sign of fucking respect, like those kids carrying Ray Liotta's groceries in *Goodfellas*."

"His mother's groceries."

"When some Norteno gets popped up in the Mission, what's the news coverage? Three sentences. Juan Valdez and his donkey were shot by Juan Marichal. The Taco Bell Chihuahua has been detained as a possible accomplice. Police are investigating. Or when Kunta Kinte shoots a wayward Theo Huxtable over in the Western Addition, there might be four sentences 'cause the media doesn't care."

"Marichal. Was he any good?"

"What a question."

"I'm trying to change the subject."

Kim stood up, a laborious process of bulk adjustments and belt pulls, and took a step toward Finch's desk. He squinted down at the photos and then picked up the notepad where Finch had written "barefoot."

He chuckled, tossed the notepad onto Finch's lap, and said, "You deserve a raise, Keanu. All these fuckers in Sacramento talking about budget crisis and cutting government jobs. If they just saw this notepad, they'd all sleep a lot better."

Kim's cell phone buzzed. He slapped at it vaguely. He said, "*Chron* is calling already—shit's about to get terrible."

"Well, then, I'm going to cut out."

"Where you headed?"

"Surfing."

"Smart man. That's gotta be the only way anyone can stay out of cell phone range in this city. There aren't even any decent tunnels."

"You could move to Marin. Drive around the hills."

Kim sounded a Bronx cheer and said, "The line of hippie tolerance ends at the Golden Gate Bridge, my friend. They'd string me up in the middle of the Mill Valley Strawberry Festival. Or they'd make me bang their ugliest women in the hopes of producing exotic kids who show aptitude at math and the violin."

"Nothing coming out of that stubby cock is going to be attractive."

"Stereotypes."

"Ugly is not a stereotype."

"You want to go interview some witnesses when you get back?"

"Sure. That sounds detectivey."

"All right, then. Go paddle out there and bust Swayze for me."

FINCH DID NOT drive to the beach. Instead, he drove down to the Mission. His wife, Sarah, poured drinks at Parea, the neighborhood's first wine bar. They had met there ten years ago. She, wearied by four years at Cal Arts and two grad years at Pratt; he, two years out of the academy and fully tanned from his newfound surfing habit. Some college friends had come into town. Finch, whose postcollegiate social life consisted almost entirely of playing poker in a local casino, was forced to consult the Internet for suggestions on what to do. The wine bar was the first place to pop up on a restaurant/nightlife review site.

He had spent most of the night sulking in the corner. His friends talked wine and asked the bartender a lot of questions about vintages and vineyards and whether or not the cheese plate was made of copper. Finch, of course, hated all of them. This fact, though, wasn't what bothered him. He had expected to hate them. Instead, he was concerned, embarrassed, really, over his hatred's easy circuitry. Was he really so simple?

When a party of overdressed Stanford grad students walked up to their booth and demanded they at least try this Malbec, Finch excused himself and walked outside. Sarah was leaning up against a bike rack, smoking a cigarette. Her hair was curlier back then and hung about her broad, octagonal head in those enviable clusters that arrange themselves, almost magnetically, with all the erratic grace of a morning glory vine.

Finch, as he usually did in the presence of beautiful women, composed his face into its most bitter iteration and said hello. She asked him how long he had known those guys in the bar. He said they were friends from college. She frowned and said that she had been positive that they were cousins or something. Who but family could make a man as tanned as Finch look so miserable?

He blushed, and in the rapid-fire, overcompensatory way shy men talk to girls who are slightly out of their league, Finch said that he couldn't recognize the neighborhood anymore. She asked if he had grown up in San Francisco. Over the next half hour, they went through the entire litany of orienting questions: Did you know so-and-so from St. Ignatius? Remember when this corner sold real ice cream? What was up with that year all the kids at Lick started wearing leather jackets? You were on the swim team? Did you know that coach who slept with the fat Getty girl?

Once the comparing of schools had exhausted its always reliable grab bag of insights, Finch found himself talking, for the first time in years, about the trips he and his mother would take down to a run-down textile store on 17th and Mission. It was the only time she held his hand, and although Finch knew, even at a young age, that the gesture shaded powerfully toward protection and almost none toward affection, he always imagined that his mother was proudly displaying their filial love to the itinerant drug addicts and prostitutes who roosted around the nearby BART station. The smell that rose up off those blocks—sun-dried piss and rotting vegetables mixed with McDonald's inimitable version of French-fried exhaust and the sinus-scraping, pungent scent of dying people—those blackening smells were his ahh smell of San Francisco. Strangely, only the memories of squalor could bring forth everything else—the cool, well-lotioned texture of his mother's palm, the sticky, hard seats of the family's tastefully old Benz, the succession of Buddhist nannies, the parties in art galleries, the Clinton fund-raisers, the Nader fund-raisers, the faint smell of peanut oil carried in the fog rolling down from the Inner Richmond, the fall afternoons spent in Golden Gate Park in the company of homeless kids with dreamy, incandescent angst, the morning swim practices in the JCC's chlorine-free pool, the endless games of Ping-Pong in the cramped student lounge at his neighborhood private school for the unmotivated children of San Francisco's liberal elite.

Sarah remembered all the same things, and although the intervening years would reveal just how differently she remembered them, at least the words used to describe those San Francisco things had matched up back then. Sometimes—most of the time—that's all it takes.

BEFORE WALKING THROUGH the front door, Finch stopped at Parea's picture window and stared in at his wife. Through the window's glare, partially obscured by the reflection of the pink and orange faces of the kooky Edwardians across the street, bathed in a synthesis of the vinegary murk that shone down from Parea's artisan skylight and the blue glow of financial news, Sarah was still the main draw, El Greco's girl in red. She leaned up against the bar, head cupped in her hands, evoking an old yet undoubtedly timeless coquettishness whose sole bene-factor was the bar's projection screen. At night, when the bar filled up with its healthy rotation of regulars, the manager played old movies off a refurbished 16-mm reel-to-reel. The nightly exposure to Ann-Margret, Kim Novak, Elizabeth Taylor, and Jayne Mansfield had filtered a se-ries of alterations into Sarah's routine gestures—her posture sagged, her speech slowed, the waistlines on her dresses crept up toward her ribs,

her lipsticks reddened. In the body of a less graceful girl, such alterations might have read as affectations, but Sarah, as she did with most
things, bludgeoned any doubts of authenticity with the certainty of her
beauty. As he watched, Finch felt, not quite subconsciously, the pleasure
of playing husband to a girl who looked like that. The slight pull—the
straightened back, the confident swing of the arms—still satisfied the
man in Finch, and, had he been able to logically sort and rank his feelings toward Sarah, the power to make him stand with better posture and
walk steadily was what he loved most about his wife.

Can any of us who have lived through love and found mostly ourselves at the end really ask for too much more?

WHEN HE FINALLY walked into Parea, Sarah did not turn around.
Finch wondered what she could possibly find interesting about the news
anchor or the litany of numbers scrolling across the bottom of the screen.
They owned no stocks or bonds or anything that might necessitate a
familiarity with or even passing interest in the greater fiscal vocabulary.

He sidled up next to her at the bar. Before she could turn to notice
him, he asked, "How's our money?"

She turned her head, slowly, and smiled.

"Didn't expect to see you down here till later."

"Got some work in the neighborhood."

"How's Jim?"

"He's a Jew today."

She paused and, with all of Hepburn's theatrics, pursed her lips, pen-
sively, before saying, "His nose is so tiny."

Finch laughed. She looked up at him. For a good second, her eyes
softened.

"I think he meant a fiscal Jew."

"I thought he just bought a Lexus."

"Nobody said he was right."

"Are you down here because of that old lady?"

"Yeah."

"I saw something on the news."

"When?"

"Couple hours ago."

"Goddammit."

"They didn't say much. Just that she was, you know, dead."

"That's it?"

"More or less. They interviewed some old Mexican lady, but the translator was terrible."

"I think I know that guy."

"The translator?"

"Yeah. He *is* awful."

"You want a drink?"

"I'm straight."

"All right. What time are you getting home?"

"Depends on the surf, I guess. Six or eight?"

"I'll pick up some bread from next door."

"Great."

FINCH DROVE A few blocks north of the housing projects on Valencia and parked his car in front of a corner Laundromat.

Because his phone told him the tide was swamping out the surf and because he wasn't hungry enough to take an early lunch, Finch sat down on a stoop across the street from the crime scene and took out his notebook. He doodled randomly: a topless Carmen Miranda on a surfboard, plunger nipples stuck straight up in the air, a snail, a martini glass. Then, bored and a bit guilty, he stood up and crossed the street to go through some investigative motions.

The yard was clean, as were both sidewalks, but in Dolores Stone's mailbox, he found a package wrapped in unmarked brown paper. On the night of the murder, a beat cop had handed Finch an armful of supermarket ads, neighborhood coalition newsletters, and credit card offers, all addressed to Stone's apartment. The exchange had been a bit strange—Finch had never seen this cop before, and although that in itself wasn't too uncommon, the cop seemed nervous and shifty. And then there was the issue of what he had said when he handed over the mail: "Here, sir, the last letters to the deceased." It was too formal a thing to say, too respectful. At the time, Finch had ascribed the beat cop's irregular behavior to his youth and, perhaps, the whiteness of the victim.

The package held a book with a plain brown cover that tried, unsuccessfully, to give the impression of leather. The title, *Mr. Brownstone*, was printed across the top in old typewriter font. There was no mention of an author or illustrator. The back cover was blank as well, as was the spine. The rest of the book, however, conformed to the usual bookish standards: a page with the Library of Congress information, an inside cover page with the title again, this time with the mark—Blacksburg Publishing—a dedication page: "To CSH." Finch recognized the title but couldn't quite place it.

Book in hand, Finch walked back to the stoop and wrote down a series of notes. A silent cheer went up in his heart as he, for the first time in many months, felt his brain unclunk. As he was drawing a mostly needless sketch of the entryway, complete with an arrow pointing out Dolores Stone's mailbox, a young woman in a black fleece exited the condo, stepped over him with an apology, smiled, and walked down to the end of the block. Finch noticed her stellar ass, of course, but then her stiff posture, the way her hands swung mechanically at her sides. He recalled one of Sarah's paintings, part of the stockades of juvenilia she kept locked up in her studio space. On an expansive spray-painted canvas, five blond girls sit in a circle around a dark wood table. Each of the girls possesses some of the traditional markings of beauty: cleavage, pearls, curls, white teeth, sloped shoulders. The girl to the extreme right has one arm laid out on the table. The girl to her left, the one with the magnificent hanging breasts, is cutting open her neighbor's wrist with a scalpel. A thick stream of blood runs down the center of the table, running in the ugly static way that things move in Frida Kahlo paintings. The expressions on the faces of all the girls, including the one being mutilated, are directly stolen off the faces of the boaters in Renoir's *The Boating Party*.

When the girl in the black fleece marched back down the block, this time with a black plastic bag from the corner store swinging arrhythmically at her side, Finch thought again of the painting and of all the girls his wife must have hated and how all their shared hatreds had hewed out an easy compatibility during those first years of marriage, and how now, as his mother had predicted, the coloration of hatred had started to fade in Sarah, leaving them with little to discuss. His work had ceased to be interesting to him. There was, and remains, no interesting way to discuss surfing with those who do not participate in the sport. She had endured ten years of similar artistic embarrassments and now relegated herself to very pretty, very well-composed paintings of buildings. Neither had any interest in music or politics, outside of what was expected of Sarah as a youngish, artsy girl in the Mission, and, as Finch had begun to realize, what was expected out of him, a trustafarian turned against his own kind.

And with that thought, he picked himself up off the stoop and started walking the two blocks over to the Porn Palace.

TODAY WE KILL, TOMORROW WE DIE

1.   I awoke at an ungodly hour, stuck in the early morning fog that loiters somewhere between consciousness and the vault of my anxieties. Whenever I find myself there, some absurd worry pokes its head out of the vagueness. This time, I worried all my friends had died in their sleep. But then Geronimo Rex dug his claws into my foot, and the panic dispersed, leaving me alone with my senses. Through the apartment's only window, I listened to two guys talk about their jobs. Some coworker wasn't showing up on time. I felt implicated, so I picked up Adam's laptop and tried to find a wireless network. But everything—belkinauto, beanmafia, loves2spooj, dukesucks, Eric's network, cafed'tazzo, thoroughbread, davis, even trusty old Linksys—was locked.

One day, when we feel a bit less embarrassed about it all, the next generation's great poet will write an elegy for the despair you feel when you, without even the hint of a password, look over a list of wireless networks and see nothing but padlocks. But until then, people like me are just going to have to feel ashamed.

I PUT ON my pants and walked down to the twenty-four-hour Laundromat/Internet café. Nobody was there save the old Chinese woman at the attendant's station. She pointed at the empty row of Internet kiosks and then at a sign. I put five dollars on the counter and sat down.

There was an e-mail from Bill admonishing me for not giving my opinion on a bukakke video and another, sent a couple minutes later, asking if I was planning on coming in to work tomorrow. I opened up the drafts folder to see if there were any e-mails I had started but never bothered to finish. I read a couple of lit blogs, but they weren't depressing enough, so I read the local news. The Baby Molester led the crime section. The story hadn't changed, save for the proliferating comments, which were all awful because they made the world seem like it was filled only with people who cared very deeply about the fate of the world.

At the bottom of the third page, there was an ad for something called the Dignity Project.

CLICK TO GO TO THE DIGNITY PROJECT. WE PROVIDE YOU WITH MORE THAN THE CHRON'S POLICY OF TURNING VICTIMS INTO STATISTICS!

I complied.

THE DIGNITY PROJECT

thedignityproject.com

... MORE THAN JUST STATISTICS

DOLORES ALLISON STONE

B: DECEMBER 15 1951. BAKERSFIELD, CA

D: MAY 12 2009. SAN FRANCISCO, CA

Dolores Allison Stone was born in Bakersfield, California, on December 15, 1951, the third child and second of twin daughters born to Frederick Jackson Stone and Elizabeth Davis Stone. Like so many young women who grew up in Southern California, Ms. Stone was drawn into acting at an early age, appearing in minor roles in a series of television sitcoms. At the age of seventeen, most likely frustrated by her seeming lack of headway in show business, Ms. Stone ran away to San Francisco, where she quickly became a Haight Street celebrity named Brown Beaver, best known for her brazen sexual exhibitionism and her revival (political) of ancient Native American dress. This second San Francisco act led to much media exposure for Ms. Stone, who most notably appeared in *Slouching Towards Bethlehem*, Joan Didion's fabled essay on Haight Street during the Summer of Love. Not much is known about Ms. Stone's life in the 70s. A marriage certificate from Modesto, California, shows that she was married to an Andrew Stein on April 5, 1975, a union that, according to state records, ended less than a year later. There are no tax records for Ms. Stone during this period.

Ms. Stone reentered the public record in 1978, when she starred in a series of adult films for Stable Abel Productions, a San

Francisco-based company led by fabled pornographer Abel Brill. According to a variety of sources, most notably Ms. Stone's much-updated livejournal.com page, she and Mr. Brill shared an on-again, off-again romance for the good part of a decade before Brill succumbed to liver cancer in 1987. Throughout that period of time, Ms. Stone appeared in over 350 Stable Abel films under a variety of aliases.

Starting in 1992, Ms. Stone worked as a volunteer at a Hunters Point orphanage. Although the details of her duties cannot be adequately confirmed, it is assumed that she did mentoring work for at-risk urban youth.

In addition to her film and philanthropic work, Ms. Stone remained actively involved in the local music scene, rejoicing in the Bay Area's wealth of concerts and festivals. Here is an excerpt from her live journal, dated December 12, 2005.

Music is everywhere! Every morning, I wake up to the sweet, somber sounds of ranchero music floating up the alley by my bedroom window. How wonderful and soul affirming to wake up to all those sad men weeping over lost loves. Then I walk out to my front stoop and hear the music of the block, the grinding of the cars, the flutterings of paper being blown over the sidewalks, the honking horns and the thump-thump of the neighborhood kids kicking soccer balls against the buildings. This is my song of San Francisco, the beautiful music of transitions and all the countries congealing together into a beautiful music. Screw the Opera, I always say, give me the moment of clarity within the chaotic music! And enjoy the chaos, too!

I stopped reading and clicked over to *Mission Dishin'*.

It had been updated. The front page now read:

BEATINGS IN MISSION LINKED TO LOCAL GANG. TECH WORKERS
TARGETED. *MISSION DISHIN'* EXCLUSIVE INTERVIEW WITH TWO
OF THE VICTIMS.

I complied.

Mission Dishin' has learned that the recent rash of savage
beatings in the Mission District are the work of the infamous Mara
Salvatrucha 13 gang, also known as the MS-13. While we are forced
to withhold certain details about the gang's intentions, for fear of
endangering more of you people, we have obtained an exclusive
interview with GLEN MARCUS (read: not his real name), one of the
victims of the attacks.

Let us set the scene: I have known Glen Marcus for years and
he has always been a tall drink of water. His demeanor, frosty, yet
compelling, might remind a casual observer of Mifune's turns in
the great Samurai films of Kurosawa. Despite this aloofness, which
has served him well, both in living in the heat of the Mission, and in
attracting his fair share of women, Marcus was savagely attacked
last weekend while walking home to our apartment on WITHHELD
and WITHHELD (far, far east of the trendy Valencia corridor). The
attackers, dressed entirely in black, beat Marcus with baseball bats.

It went on like that for another three paragraphs. Glen Marcus, predictably, was a fucking idiot. He had suffered a broken arm, a fractured

skull, and abrasions on his knees and elbows. They had taken his wallet, his phone. The reason why he suspected the Mara Salvatrucha 13 was because they were wearing blue and had done things like this in the past.

The only evidence offered to corroborate the MS-13 theory came from the editors of *Mission Dishin'*. Apparently, they had been in contact with three of the victims (there had been about eight in all), and all three had worked for prominent but not Google-prominent companies in Silicon Valley. All three companies could be described as "social media."

I admit, the last part gave me pause. To deflect some of the accusations that we were nothing but a $50 leech on heartbroken men, the founder of getoverit.com had registered us as a social networking site.

Were the letters from Richard McBeef some weird intimidation tactic? Why would the MS-13, who I assumed were drug dealers, suddenly move into low-level terrorist activities?

Below the byline, there was a link to the San Francisco Gang Prevention Society's website. I clicked on it. All it was, really, was a phone number and a collection of other links. The other links, though, confirmed Performance Fleece's worst plausible scenario. The evidence— descriptions of citizen intimidation, initiation rituals, neighborhood blog posts about knifings, muggings gone wrong—proved, indisputably, really, that we were both fucked. My right hand throbbed uncontrollably. I clicked through hundreds of photos—all those proud kids posing in red, the brutal accounts of violence, the efficiency of gang logic. My panic now had a face, hundreds of them. When the sun finally came up and the fresh-faced morning people started coming into the Laundromat with their loads for the wash-and-fold service, I had already known, for several hours, really, that I could never go back to my apartment.

2.   When I walked into the office, Bill was sitting at my desk. He said his computer had a virus. We both knew he was lying. He just liked my desk better because he's that sort of guy. Flattery kept my mouth shut.

Bill said, "I can't get rid of this."

"What?"

"This pop-up. It's on my shit, too."

"That's that giant."

"The Big Friendly Giant. Roald Dahl."

"What's he doing?"

"I have no idea. Just sitting there. Being gay."

"Is there a movie coming out?"

"Already checked."

"You can't get rid of it?"

"I've been trying for thirty minutes."

"What are you doing on my computer, anyway?"

"Looking for a job."

I looked over my shoulder and made the international sign for "Do you have any weed, and if you do, can I smoke some?"

Bill nodded and motioned with his head toward the elevator.

It was a coin flip: either the weed would make me so paranoid that I would have to figure out what to do about the Baby Molester and the Advanced Creative Writer, or that pleasant fog would set in and I'd find things funny and any decision could be delayed. Either way.

3. New Montgomery Street was surprisingly empty for an hour so close to lunch. We walked toward our usual alleyway on Minna. On the corner of Mission and 6th, we saw Frank Chu, the city's most famous protester, the man who *SF Weekly* had named the city's Best Pathological Citizen, silently holding up his black and neon sign.

Today, it read:

MENARD

475,000 GALAXIES

ZEGNATRONIC

AWTROCENTENNIAL

CBS: JUXTAGRONIKUL BROADCASTS

As we walked by, Bill raised up a fist and screamed, "Fuck CBS!" Frank Chu looked at us through his aviators and shrugged. Today was just another day in his interminable war, I guess. For the past fifteen years, while trudging around Montgomery Street, he had been calling for the impeachment of Bill Clinton. Chu believed that Clinton had once greenlighted a television show called *The Richest Family*, which had covertly documented the lives of Chu and his family. According to Wikipedia, Chu believed that Clinton was working on behalf of the 12 Galaxies conspiracy, the interplanetary organization that had profited wildly off of *The Richest Family*.

Chu's demands: the impeachment of President Clinton and $20 billion in damages for the humiliation inflicted upon him and his family by the 12 Galaxies conspiracy. To help supplement his daily protests,

Chu sold ad space on the back of his sign for $100 a week. Today, he was hocking Quizno's new Tuscan Ranch chicken sandwich.

TWO SFMOMA STAFFERS were cracking whip-its in our smoking alley. I recognized them by their butchered haircuts and the ambient green badges pinned to their black uniforms.

When they finally left, giggling and superior, Bill and I huddled in their vacated space. We passed around the bowl and talked about a couple of bands and I brought up Ronizm and Bill accused me of being boring because I never really talked about anything other than hip-hop from the nineties and I reminded Bill that the reason why this happened was because he never wanted to talk about anything but how much he hated our job and, when that became overbearing, music. It wasn't a bad time. The coin flip, at least to date, was going my way. The SFMOMA staffers came back with more whip-its and matching cups of frozen yogurt. We passed the bowl around again. They cracked some whip-its. Between balloons, I told them about the Baby Molester and they cautioned me, more implored me, to not go seek the police. The SFMOMA staffers lived in Outer Excelsior, which was like the supergrimy Mission, and they knew some things about what happens to snitches.

When we got back to work, the Google transplants were standing in our kitchen, stealing our cereal, watching the new *Family Feud*. Bill e-mailed me my day's work and went off to go harass the Google guys.

FROM: RICHARD MCBEEF <rmcbeef@elsewhere.net>
TO: PHILIP DAVIS <phil@getoverit.com>

Philip,

It is great to hear from you. Yes, the pressures of IT are immeasurable, especially what with these assholes treating you like a slave. Hope your friend from college is over his particular bitch. Where did you go to college? You don't have to be specific, but I went to school at a small college in New England and my perspective on things has changed a lot as a result. Just wanted to know if the guy I was paying for here came from a similar place.

Thanks,
Rich

Richard McBeef again? I still couldn't imagine why Adam would pay $50 for a joke he just as easily could have sent over e-mail. All non-Adam-related explanations were too weird, too coincidental. I put it out of my mind.

Mostly, the responses to follow-up e-mails were attempts to recoup the $50 credit card charge. A good percentage of them tried to explain the initial e-mail as a prank by friends at either a bachelor party or a college reunion. We were instructed to respond by cutting and pasting part of the agreement form they had clicked on, which stated that all sales were final. However, in our goodwill, we were supposed to offer a $5 credit for any future uses of the site. The few customers who followed up to our follow-up were either lawyers, insane, or suicidal. We were instructed to strongly urge them to seek out psychiatric help and consult the Internet to see if a conflict of medications might be causing an abnormal mood swing. Then, as gently as fast will allow, we were instructed to get the fuck out of Dodge.

It was rare to get a follow-up e-mail that asked specific questions and actually tried to use the advertised service. Anyway, I wrote him back.

FROM: PHILIP DAVIS <Phil@getoverit.com>
TO: RICHARD MCBEEF <rmcbeef@elsewhere.net>

Hey Rich,

Good to hear from you. Thank God, that friend of mine who worked in IT and got snaked by his bitch has gotten over it. It's the only reason why we're still friends today. Weird you mention it, but I did go to a small college in New England, and much like you, it did help shape a lot of how I see the world. Good to know we're a good match off the start.

Write me back at your leisure. Till then, I would say that New England guys always have a tough time showing emotions. Allow yourself to show emotions.

Sincerely,
Philip

I found Bill in the kitchen with the Google guys. Someone was trying to figure out how to open the window. There was a lengthy discussion about windows in office buildings and insurance and the sound a body must make when it hits cement after a fifteen-story fall. We all watched the rest of *Family Feud*, said good-bye, and headed off to the bar.

It was only two-thirty, but the bartender agreed to start happy hour a half hour early. Bill and I bitched about the Google transplants, talked to the bartender about funny commercials, and drank down a few pints. When the mass of people who had jobs like us flooded the bar at around three-thirty, we took a cab down to the Mission. Bill knew a few girls who were going to be at a bar. He promised, unnecessarily, really, that each one of them was hot.

They weren't, but they asked a lot of questions and had encouraging things to say about writing and the creativity process. Bill had clearly lied to them about our work. It was okay, though. The room was spinning, and the second hottest girl was buying me drinks and yelling something about wanting to work in microfinance if only she could find something she truly believed in. I think, at some point, I went to the bathroom and threw up and put Sam Cooke on the jukebox and might have even danced with my second-hottest casualty of capitalism and goodwill.

The bar closed down. I didn't know where to go and the second hottest girl punched her number in my phone and disappeared with her friends. Bill offered me his couch, but I waved him off and headed off in the general direction of Adam's apartment.

4.   I stumbled toward 16th. After a long night of drinking, I usually find myself at whatever taquería or pizzería will have me. That night, as the soft edges of a blackout crept over my vision, I remember craving a jalapeño slice at the old hippie pizza parlor that was now run by doughnut tycoon Cambodians. I am a very dark shade of Korean, a fact that was the subject of years and years of family jokes, and I always had the feeling that the polite service afforded to my drunken ass by the Cambodians might come from an ethnic misunderstanding on their part. As I rounded Shotwell and 18th, a man in black stepped out from behind a relic of a station wagon. He was wearing a black ski mask and black gloves.

I remember crossing the street. Another man, dressed identically, materialized from behind a hedgerow. He had something that looked like a remote control in his right hand. My fate seemed inevitable. But just as I was getting psyched to take a punch, the man behind the hedgerow jabbed me in the chest with his remote control and the edges of my vision went from numb to electric blue. When I was done convulsing around, one of the two men stepped down hard on my neck. In a calm and even voice, he said, "We will not allow you to corrupt our society any longer. All vermin will be silenced. The lion will rise again."

5. The police had no idea what the hell anything meant. They suggested I might be imagining things. They pointed out that my phone had not been stolen, which, according to them, explained everything. They asked if I had health insurance, and when I laughed, they offered me a ride to Adam's.

Adam had his own theory.

"It was David."

"Who?"

"The Advanced Creative Writer."

"Oh no."

"Think. The confrontation on your block, the talk about silence. The heightened, weird diction, and the lion."

"The lion?"

"This kid always writes about this fucked-up hierarchy of animals. Lions are the highest. I always imagined it was gang symbolism."

"Oh no."

"You're sure he said 'all vermin will be silenced'?"

"Pretty sure. Sixty percent sure."

"That's right in his linguistic wheelhouse. His characters all talk like extras in a Goebbels biopic."

"Oh no."

His logic was unassailable. I was screwed. All the Advanced Creative Writer would have to do was look up Adam's address on the school's directory and I would be caught. But where to go? Adam was my number one friend in the city, Bill my number two. I couldn't think of a number three; I suppose if someone held a gun up to my head, I'd say Performance Fleece. If the Advanced Creative Writer had been following me around that night and had any access to social networking sites, he would know all the peripheral details of Bill.

If he could find Bill, he could find me, and all my thirty-seven Internet friends.

I left Adam's, despite his deflated protests. At a dollar store across the street, I bought two pairs of socks, a packet of boxer shorts, and a plastic cutlery set. Then, with a weight on my heart alternating between heavy and giddy, I walked into the lobby of the Hotel St. Francis.

BOOK TWO

Finch walked up 14th. Erected in 1912 during the city's great rebuilding campaign after the earthquake of 1906, the 200,000-square-foot building now known as the Porn Palace served for seventy-four years as an armory for the National Guard. In 1976, the National Guard transferred its operations down south to Fort Funston, and the armory, a block-swallowing Borg of a building, was abandoned to the city's skateboarders, who converted the front stairs into a spot called Three Up–Three Down. The fate of the building was left in the hands of competing community concerns, which meant that it was left to rot, save for a short period of time when George Lucas drove his trucks across the Bay Bridge and filmed some of *Star Wars* in the old armory's drill court.

In 2006, after thirty years of inaction and mounting disrepair, one of the community concerns won out. A pornographer specializing in BDSM and niche films purchased the old armory, citing the building as the ideal place to house his studios. The building was redubbed the Porn Palace.

To the right of the Porn Palace's studded Moorish front door, Finch noticed a small white placard that read PLEASE PUSH BUTTON. The location of the button was pointed out by a friendly blue arrow. Finch pushed the button. A woman's voice, transmitted through some unseen speaker, asked, "Hello?"

Finch said, "Hello."

"Can I help you?"

"SFPD. I'm here about Dolores Stone."

"Who?"

"Dolores Stone."

"I heard that, but who are you?"

"SFPD."

"SFPD who?"

"Sid Finch. SFPD. Homicide."

"Coming right down."

While he waited, Finch flashed through a series of fantasies about the woman who was coming right down. Would she be a black drag queen wearing some jewel-encrusted, solid-gold bikini? A six-foot-nine Amazon in leather? A petite Asian girl whose monstrous implants doubled as a double-barreled fuck-you to the Hippocratic oath? Just as he was measuring out the contours of the Asian girl's cookie nipples, the door swung open, revealing a woman who, unfortunately, sat squarely within his expectations of the women of San Francisco. Finch, still pricked up by his prior expectations, gave her the up and down, starting at her Chinese-ish shoes, her pale, follicle-stippled legs streaked pink from a careless shave, the soft bulge of thigh hanging unathletically over well-scrubbed knee. The heavy, two-tone skirt—cordovan and a deep purple—hung stiffly and unevenly from sharp hips, revealing a flash of midriff that ended at the hem of an overwrought, vaguely African halter top. A wooden bead held the neck together. Her mousy hair had been butchered straight across her forehead before giving way to two wings that hung damply over her ears. She was ugly, of course, but like so many of San Francisco's ugly girls, she buried the fact behind an earnest expression, as if every doorway was a wardrobe and the entirety of Narnia lay across the threshold.

"Come on up," she said. "Miles has been expecting you."

MILES HOFSPAUR, ENTREPRENEUR, sat behind an industrial desk in a bare room on the second floor. Again, Finch felt let down. Where was the approximation of Hefner life, the blond twins, the stained casting couch? Hofspaur—bald, blotchy, unevenly hefted—was dressed in a tight black T-shirt that barely hemmed in his bulk. He stood up and shook Finch's hand. On the desk, Finch noticed a drawing, not quite finished: Lisa Simpson, on her knees, holding Bart's snail cock in her hand. Through a feat of neck contortion only allowed by 2-D, the viewer could see Lisa's face, the look of tired guilt. Were there a speech bubble sprouting from her now-defiled mouth, it would have read, "I guess you caught us, so what are you going to do?"

In a nasally, giggly voice, Hofspaur said, "Sorry."

"They look old."

"Those early seasons were the best seasons."

Finch didn't really see what that had to do with anything, but he asked, "What's with the look on her face?"

"That, believe it or not, is the product of market research. Our research team said that this sort of cartoon shit does better when the girl looks like she isn't really enjoying what's going on." He paused, waited for Finch to respond, and when Finch said nothing, said, "Sorry, it's sick, I know, but it's not kiddie porn because there's no victim, right?"

"Yes."

"You know what's really fucked up? We can do whatever we want to Lisa Simpson or Dora the Explorer or Minnie Mouse, but if we Photoshop footage from nonanimated sitcoms, the feds immediately start sending us e-mails. We ran this Rudy Huxtable reverse interracial series a couple years ago, and I swear we almost got shut down."

Finch, despite himself, chuckled.

Hofspaur sat back down behind his desk and folded his hands, regally, in his lap. He asked, "What do you want to know about Dolores?"

"Anything that seems relevant."

"Relevant? Her stage name was Gray Beaver, for the obvious reasons, but also because she was a quarter Potawatomi and incorporated some weird Indian shit in her videos."

"Gray Beaver?"

"Yeah. You know, 'cause she had a gray beaver."

"Yes."

"You're a bit slow for a detective there."

"Sorry. I don't have my notebook with me."

Hofspaur laughed. Recently, it had been going like this for Finch.

"Can you think of anyone who would want to hurt her?"

"Not really. None of the red flags that come up for other girls ever came up for her. Even her fan mail was, dare I say, conversational."

"Conversational?"

Hofspaur let out a faint Bronx cheer.

"Yeah, like they were just usual fan stuff. Where did she grow up, what orifice she likes the best, if she likes black cock or white cock. Actually, I would say half of her mail came from this scene in a remake of *Dances with Wolves* where she blew smoke signals out of her twat."

"How?"

"That's what the letters were asking."

Finch grunted.

"But yes, nothing alarming. Actually, we have someone from your department come in and teach the girls how to spot potential problems. Like a certain tone in a letter or something like that."

"Do you have the name of this officer?"

"Bar Davis."

"Bar?"

"I think it's short for Barbara."

"Okay."

"Do you want to borrow a sheet of paper to write down that name?" He held up the drawing of Lisa Simpson.

Although he hated to kowtow to any sordid thing, this second viewing of Lisa Simpson, defiled, turned Finch's stomach. Not because he felt the need to piously hawk over the idols of his childhood, but rather, because the drawing reminded him of Sarah. Even after finishing at the academy, when most of the convictions of youth are hammered over by the mantra of serve and protect, Finch still put his faith in the following equation: "I, Siddhartha Finch, love *The Simpsons*. Everything I find funny can be found somewhere in the first seven seasons of the show. Humor is important to human relationships. Therefore, if anyone born in America between 1970 and 1986 does not like or 'get' *The Simpsons*, he/she and I will be missing an integral component to human relationships. Only unhappiness can follow."

On their third date, Finch, giddied by a mention of Space Camp, rattled off a not quite relevant "It's like that *Simpsons* when Homer did *x*" monologue. Sarah's bemused but undeniably uncomprehending reaction—fluttering eyelids, a smile, mouth half open—hurt him, sure, but the prettiness with which she did it made him reconsider the idealism of his youth.

Ten years had passed since the third date, and here he was, staring down a distance without contours, wondering if he had sold out the Simpsons Compatibility Equation to install the always-maturing, yet thoroughly compromised steps in his career of love.

It was a moment he had expected to have at some point. Just not quite this early.

Eyes downcast, he said, "Put that down."

Hofspaur complied.

Summoning a little more bass in his voice, Finch asked, "So, there were no danger signs in her letters?"

"No."

"All right. Thanks."

"Detective."

"Yes."

"Do you want the letters?"

"Have there been any threatening letters, anything out of the ordinary?"

"Only the usual crap from the stupid cyberpunk cult."

"Cyberpunk cult?"

HOFSPAUR LED FINCH down a sterile hallway to a room lined with industrial shelving. Inside a banker's box were hundreds of letters composed entirely with words cut out from newspapers and magazines. In vague, unimaginative language, they detailed the misfortune that would befall the reader if he or she did not stop his or her immoral activity.

As Finch read through a handful, Hofspaur dug in the files until he came up with a letter that had been composed on a sheet of yellow legal paper. He slid it on top of the letters already in Finch's hand.

Dear GRAY Beaver

You are a SLUTS. IF you do not CEASE AND DESIST with your behavior, we will come for you. You are befouling this city with your INSANE DEPRAVITY. We are SERIOUS. STOP immediately and GET YOUR ASS off the fucking INTERNET.

YOU know who THIS is.

Finch asked, "Are they Christians or something?"

Hofspaur chortled and shook his head. "No. They're not Christians. I don't even know what the fuck to call them. They're like communist Buddhist vegan assholes. Who all happen to be ex-hackers."

"Ex-hackers?"

"And it begins again. . . . Yes. Ex-hackers. They all purified themselves or some bullshit and now decry the Internet as some filthy black hole designed to suck people's life away from them. So, like all good little *Star Wars*–bred rebels, they fuck up sites like us, dating sites, social networking, et cetera."

"Huh."

"At the beginning, they could hack in and mess with our shit, at least for a few hours, but they haven't been able to get around our security for a few years now."

"These hackers, do you know what they call themselves?"

"The Brownstone Knights."

"That's it?"

"Yeah. Pretty fucking lame."

"How do you know about all this?"

"They have a website."

Hofspaur pulled out his phone, fiddled around with it, and pushed it in front of Finch's nose. The website was ugly: all-black background, pine-green text, with two distorted photos of the storefront, a weather-beaten Victorian standing alone amid a lagoon of cement and chain-link fencing.

The green text read:

At the BEING ABUNDANCE CAFETERIA, we honor the abundance of the earth and ourselves, as we are one and the same. To that end, we do not believe in any separations, between animals and humans, between men and women, between races, religions, creeds, or class. Instead, we believe in BEING ABUNDANCE, a concept engineered by our founding couple, the indefatigable, bountiful Siobahn Menglehart and Jacky Stoddard. The core values of BEING

ABUNDANCE encompass Love & Acceptance, Generosity, Worth, Gratitude and Creation or Responsibility. We believe the practice of BEING ABUNDANCE starts with what we put into our bodies. For tens of thousands of generations, humans have sanctified and ritualized both what and how we eat. We, at the BEING ABUNDANCE CAFETERIA, believe in the lessons of real history and therefore have created a space where San Franciscans can engage in the food act in a noncommercialized and noncompromised way. To achieve this purity, we gather our bounty from only organic, local growers, who, in turn, only use environmentally sustainable practices, as these are the best way we can truly honor the earth. We invite you to step inside and enjoy being someone that chooses: loving your life, adoring yourself, accepting the world, being generous and grateful every day, and experiencing being provided for. Have fun and enjoy being nourished!

Finch winced. He had never been able to stomach the combination of disorganized and optimistic things, especially to this extent. Turning to Hofspaur, he said, "How do you know the cyberpunks are affiliated with this?"

"Have you ever been to Being Abundance?"

"No."

"Have you eaten lunch yet?"

THE WAITRESSES AT the Being Abundance Cafeteria were all beautiful and slouchy and bandanna-ed. An odd, reddish sheen radiated off each one's cheeks. At first, Finch wrote it off as a trick of light, but as he looked around at the other customers cooped up in the long, narrow railroad apartment of a seating area, he noticed that everyone else, including Hofspaur, who, back at the Porn Palace, had been pink as the bottom of an infant's foot, looked a little gray. At a long blond wood bar near the front entrance, five men sat *Nighthawks* style, drinking down some green liquid.

There was something off about the men as well, nothing as noticeable as the waitresses, but similar to the unsettled sensation you get when you take money out of the ATM and the bills, which you rationally know are not counterfeit, nonetheless feel a bit too gritty in your fingers. After a quick up and down, Finch realized that the fabric of their shirts was a bit too airy and light. Despite the lack of open windows or doors, each of the men's sleeves fluttered in some unseen wind.

Upon walking through the front door, Hofspaur and Finch had been greeted by one of three brunettes, all of whom had short-cropped, bowly hair. Like all the other girls, she had that reddish sheen. Her eyes, Finch noticed, were set a bit wider apart than one would usually expect in a human being. In a voice bearing the full benefit of healthy lungs and good posture, she said, "Welcome to the Being Abundance Cafeteria. Would you like to hear the question of the day?"

Hofspaur, sniggering, said, "Please."

"What future are you living toward?"

"White power, brother."

"Excuse me?" Her eyes darted over to a small, bedazzled icon of President Barack Obama that had been pasted up on the cash register.

"White powder," Hofspaur said. "Trying to kick a habit. Hoping the future is free of white powder."

Relief flooded over her face. She touched her finger to her clavicle and said, "Well, I wish you all the best of luck with that. Everything you put into your body goes into your body."

"This is true. Can you bring us two bee pollen smoothies, please?"

"You Are Vivacious. Amanda will be right over to take your food order. While you wait, enjoy the artwork and please, feel free to play the Abounding River Game."

A series of paintings had been hung up on the walls. Scanned from left to right, a narrative line revealed itself. A young blond girl with pigtails stands behind a brick wall. It is raining. On the other side of the wall, which appears to have been constructed at a forty-five-degree angle, the grass is green, rabbits stare impassively at pink flowers. A row of trees gamely hold on to their gigantic fruit. In the second painting, the girl, digging in the hard, ugly dirt on her side of the brick wall, comes across a small white box. The next few paintings show the girl opening the box, which contains a red apple and a glowing scroll.

In the last five paintings, the girl eats the apple, reads the scroll. The wall dissolves, and the girl enters the bountiful paradise.

On each table in Being Abundance, there was a basket filled with crayons, dice, and greeting-card-size reproductions of each of the paintings. On the backs of the cards were instructions on things to say to the people at your table, and, if you had procured prior consent, the people at the next.

Hofspaur flipped through the cards and grunted. "These idiots couldn't even make the game complicated."

"What would be the point of that?"

The hostess came by with the drinks, which were a radioactive shade of green.

"Well, it would at least have some allure to it."

Finch felt a tingly lift at the base of his scalp. To mask whatever his face was giving away, he scowled at his green drink and announced, "This thing tastes pretty toxic."

"That means it's working. As I was saying, the game is so simple, as are these ugly communist paintings, because these idiots want to sell a linear path to happy. But the trick only works on people who are already happy. No miserable fuck wants to wake up one morning and realize that salvation is just an easy twelve-step jaunt down a path that's been obvious the entire time. The straight line demeans their intelligence, their families, and all the fucked-up psychological trauma that brought them to their particular misery."

"And yet this place is crowded at eleven-fifteen on a Tuesday."

"People who refuse to respect traditional mealtimes are all happy. Or something like that."

"I don't think that works."

"Sure it does. If you don't really feel your misery or if it doesn't exist, you can walk right out of it. That's the accidental genius of this place. They make a bunch of nine-dollar drinks, sell a bunch of fucking horse food for twenty-five dollars, tacitly remind rich people of the possibility of misery, and then advertise a way out of it. It's essentially allowing the happy to be temporarily confused about being happy and then showing them that all they have to do is be happy and think that the world is exactly what it is to the rich and happy."

"What's that?"

"A bountiful place. A place where the ears of corn are huge and the fucking blacks and Mexicans and Chinese and retarded don't venture, even though they are welcome. There's no net effect, except that someone paid nine dollars for a drink and twenty-five dollars for a plate of seaweed and someone pocketed that money. But no matter, there's plenty more for nine-dollar drinks and twenty-five-dollar plates of seaweed. Keep it simple. Remind rich people that all they have to do to remind themselves that they aren't miserable is to look in the mirror."

"You don't think they do this on purpose?"

"What does on purpose even mean? Everyone here, they're all fundamentally happy people who need this"—he turned his palms up to the ceiling and gestured, disgustedly, at the paintings—"to temporarily displace their happiness, so they can discover it again. Anything rich people like: hiking in the outdoors, crossword puzzles, fucking opera, art galleries, volunteer work, domestic literary fiction, surfing, John Updike—it's all the same: bullshit engineered to make people bored and kinda miserable until they finish, at which point they can allow themselves to feel satisfied for walking the straight line."

Finch couldn't help himself. He was beginning to really like Hofspaur. He announced, "I surf."

"That's a bit surprising."

"Why?"

"Because you, more than any other cop I've ever met, are an ulcerous, miserable fuck."

"That's a bit presumptuous, no?"

"An old woman gets murdered in an area of the Mission rife with gang violence during one of the worst gang wars in the city's history. You, the detective assigned to the case, are sitting at a cultish restaurant with the city's nastiest pornographer, investigating inefficient cyberpunks."

A red-faced brunette came around to Finch and Hofspaur's table and asked if they were ready to order. Finch, quickly studying the menu, said he'd have the sampler plate. A beatific glow glazed over the girl's eyes. Bowing her head, she said, "You are diverse."

"The sampler plate."

"You are diverse."

Hofspaur pointed at the menu: Next to the description of the sampler plate were the words "I AM DIVERSE." Every item on the menu had a different, loosely relevant affirmation.

"I am diverse."

"You are diverse."

Hofspaur chuckled and announced, "I am fertile."

The waitress bowed again and said, "You are fertile," before smiling and shuffling away.

Just then, the five men at the bar jerked up to their feet. The one with the most interesting facial hair stood front and center, while the other four fanned out behind him. In an effete, squeaky voice, he asked, "Are you Miles Hofspaur?"

Hofspaur raised an eyebrow and smirked at Finch.

The man jabbed Hofspaur's shoulder with an insistent finger. "I am talking to you. Please pay me the respect of an answer. Are you Miles Hofspaur?"

Hofspaur said, "Doctor Hofspaur, please."

"You are not welcome here, Doctor Hofspaur. Please leave."

"Excuse me?"

"You are not welcome here. Please leave."

"This is America. I can sit here and eat your food and pay you money."

The man who was doing the jabbing paused to solemnly close his eyes. Then, recomposed, he jabbed Hofspaur in the shoulder again.

Hofspaur said, "What is illegal, by the way, is assault."

Finch kind of grunted. Again, the light tingle started at the base of his skull, but this time it felt more insistent. He thought of the scene in the movie *Akira* where Tetsuo balloons out into a breathing, blinking globe of blood vessels and eyes.

"I will stop when you leave."

"I already ordered, fuckhead. I'll leave when you stop sending your lame letters to my business."

"I don't know what you're referring to, but if you do not leave, I will be forced to call the police."

Hofspaur laughed derisively and pointed at Finch, who was trying to hide his face behind what remained of his green drink. "That," he said, pointing at Finch, "is the police."

"Well, then the officer should be well versed that this is a private establishment and that we reserve the right to serve who we want to serve, and that in this case, we refuse to serve people who relocate men and women from the bounty of the earth into the wasteland of depravity and virtual death found on websites like smut.com and its affiliated websites."

Everyone turned to look at Finch, who, in turn, stared into the bottom of his glass. He became acutely aware of the empty space underneath his armpit where his holster usually would be.

The man closest to Finch, who, had this been a boy band, might have been the forgettable baritone, asked, "Officer, what's the verdict?"

The tingling intensified. It almost felt as if the back of his head was slowly being sheared off. It occurred to him that he might have been drugged. But when he looked over at Hofspaur, he didn't notice any discomfort on his new friend's face.

"Do you own this place?" Finch heard himself ask.

"This is a collective. It is owned by the workers."

A digitized whomping flooded Finch's ears—a loud, vibrating noise, which, had he been able to access his memory, he might have recognized as the sound you hear after huffing down a canister of nitrous oxide. His vision blurred. He was vaguely aware of some danger. At some point, he began to laugh. His cheeks felt enormous. A wet sensation splashed across his thighs.

Then, as easy as that, he blacked out.

LET'S ALL SAVE
TONY ORLANDO'S HOUSE

1.   And so I began my stay at the Hotel St. Francis under the name Charlie Dushu. For an extra $20 a week, I was given my own bathroom and daily maid service, which meant at ten every morning, my neighbor would knock politely on our shared door. On the first morning, she waddled in, knock-kneed, approximated a service smile, and proceeded to punch the pillows and toss the shabby brown comforter over the unspeakable mattress. The next day, she took out the trash. She was about nineteen, maybe eighteen, and didn't really say much to me.

What would be the point of describing her build, the color of her hair, the shape of her eyes? Just know, I tipped her well.

Most of the social activity at the Hotel St. Francis occurred inside the shared bathrooms, so it was kind of like high school in that way. Tenants did congregate in the lobby, but only to succumb, collectively, to their catatonia. The TV didn't get VH1. Or *SportsCenter*. I could sense everyone's hatred. On the first day, I sat in my room and read *Hunger*, which I hoped would put things in the proper perspective. It didn't work.

After an hour of deliberation, I called my favorite Chinese delivery place and demanded they bring the food directly to my room.

When the delivery guy got to the lobby, he called my cell phone and pretended to not speak English until I agreed to come downstairs. He must have recognized me from earlier deliveries because he frowned, not in sympathy or anger, but rather in concentration, as he did the math we all do when we are confronted with the irrefutable proof of debits and hard times.

I tipped him well, too.

I don't know if it was the smell of Lunch Combo 21 or the sound of cash exchanging hands, but the bodies in the green lawn chairs all sat up and turned their heads in our direction. The delivery guy frowned again. I knew what he was thinking: Whatever you've done, you deserve what's coming.

One of the bodies lifted itself out of its chair and staggered on over.

It was my disenfranchised friend from Election Day, the one who looked like Cornel West, but with bits of doughnut in his beard. He asked if I remembered him.

It never occurred to me that the insane might be able to recognize actual people.

He asked again, "Hey, do you remember me?"

"The election."

"That's right. You stood beside me as we made history together!"

He grabbed my wrists. His palms felt like the palms of a scholar, clammy and smooth. I worried about my food, the possibility of contamination.

When it became clear that I had nothing to say, he said, "If we don't have the ability to separate ourselves from ourselves and use that one good part of ourselves to make a statement via the political process, no matter the results, then we really are slaves. You know that, right?"

I managed to slip my wrists away from his hands. He frowned and, with the care of a surgeon, plucked Lunch Combo 21 out of my hands, placed it on a nearby table, and regrabbed my wrists.

He asked, "Do you support the revolution?"

"Sure."

2.   I admit: Being surrounded by desperation eased my panic, or, at least, it displaced it for a while. In retrospect, it's clear that in an effort to place itself in familiar surroundings, my mind had simply transposed the sympathetic desperation of the characters in my favorite books, songs, and movies onto the depleted bodies that shuffled by in the lobby. Cornel West with food in his beard became a synthesis of the dying Ronizm, three, maybe four characters from *A Confederacy of Dunces,* with Laurence Fishburne's character in *Searching for Bobby Fischer* mixed in for good measure. The girl who cleaned my room every morning was not a tragically young heroin addict, but rather, Camilla, Arturo Bandini's Mexican lover from *Ask the Dust.* As such, whenever she came by, I mourned for her as if she were dying somewhere in the desert, her life mortgaged out to some worthless mope.

It's been brought to my attention by several people, who, if I am being kind to myself, have a genuine concern for my well-being, that this state of affairs does not deviate much from my usual approach to life. I suppose it might be true. Maybe all my Colleens and Kathleens and Lauras were just variations of Old Jane from *The Catcher in the Rye* or whatever character Zooey Deschanel happened to be playing in a movie, every street corner I drive past will forever be Queensbridge '85, but even if this is true and I live in a shadow, contingent world, I've never been able to summon up, as we used to say in high school debate, an impact to this scenario.

3.   On the ninth morning of my stay, I went with James to the library. He needed someone with good standing to log him into the computer terminals. Nobody else qualified, he explained. I found this a bit hard to believe, but I had nothing else to do.

I've worked in libraries and therefore know that deranged homeless men have only two uses for the Internet: the lottery and porn. Thankfully, James chose the former, although I will admit, when I first looked over at his screen lit up with numbers and charts, a little hope flared up, however briefly and nostalgically, that perhaps James was some discarded savant, and that his way, whatever that might be, would be the one for me. But then he ferreted greedily into his pocket and pulled out a fistful of Lotto tickets.

I went back to checking my e-mail.

There was nothing from work. I read through a couple of blogs, aimlessly typing in the URLs of sites I had visited before—the same mean-spirited celebrity gossip sites, the same baseball stat nerd blogs, the same photo blogs manned by gay men who shared my love for pale, big-eyed brunettes, the same true crime reports.

As James thwacked away at his forehead, stunned at every loss, I found myself stalking the Baby Molester. The Dignity Project profile had not been updated. There was a lengthy *Chronicle* article, but it just rearranged the available information into tighter sentences and shorter paragraphs. Combining her name with several different keywords yielded not much else, although I did learn that there was a Dolores Stone who sang and played tambourine in a psychedelic band called the Terror of the Smallpox Blankets.

There was no choice left. I read her blog.

MARCH 20 2008

The future president, Presidential, addresses the waiting nation on the squawk box tonight, regarding the charges brought up by one Jeremiah Wright. We shall pause in bestowing on Mr. Wright what he believes to be his God-Given title of Reverend until he shows us some Reverential (hell, we'd even settle for Christian) actions. The we, here, refers to those of us who, through blood, sweat and tears, have withstood the earth, wind and fire of injustice, those of us who earned our judgment. Not the sheltered do-gooder poseurs, hiding in their hooded sweatshirts, grandstrutting about the streets of San Francisco, handing out pamphlets to the already-initiated, both sides sunning themselves in the freedom we worked so hard to provide, using words like change, liberation, break the order, the same words we used back when those words mattered. Now they just sound like they were bought at the mall. I would stop and blow up their preconceptions, but I have neither the time, nor the inclination to explain the truth to someone who rises and shines under the sun of freedom we provided for them. . . .

Next.

MARCH 18 2008

Winston R. Pummelstein, as he's known to those in the know, came by today with a stack of our old records. I put our first recording on the old Victrola and with that first twang of Gusto's guitar, ringing out the revolution, the walls fell away from my living room, modest, simple, furnished by Salvation Army, and we were back in '72, in similar digs. I could see it all: me, stomping around, trying to not be Janis, but with Janis always on my mind; Gusto: his handbands and his rituals; Winston: fat, gold and shiny.

Pummelstein is in a bad way. His mind is just hanging on, I can tell. The music must have transported him back, just like it did me. He must not be seeing what I see whenever I look in the mirror or whenever Miles forces me to watch some cut of one of my movies. I see the awesome power of gravity. His mind is so fucked with acid that he must be seeing these tits when they defied Newton and this ass back when even the Panthers would call it sweet.

I began to cry. For the first time in years, I thought about a friend of mine named Hal who had worked with me in the library at Bowdoin. My freshman year, I'd invite Hal up to my room to smoke pot and stream underground hip-hop over the Internet. At some point that spring, the resident adviser put an end to it. Apparently, one of the girls in the hall thought it was sketchy to have a "townie who doesn't even go here" hanging out in the dorms.

I wrote the girl a letter whose contents don't need to be mentioned ever again. The resident adviser's punishment? In the cafeteria, I held a reading of the poetry he had published in the school's literary journal. It sufficed.

As for Hal, I began hanging out with him at his apartment across the bridge in Topsham. One of his friends lived in a hallway closet, the other slept on the couch. They were, I admit, ravers. But nobody at Bowdoin would do the drugs I wanted to do, and so I, too, for a period of about six months, became a raver. Hal's parents were hard-burned Deadheads who owned a pasta shop up near campus. From them, he inherited a heavy hand with garlic and a belief in roving, ecstatic tribalism. Before my first rave, outside of a tool and die factory in Athol, Massachusetts, Hal handed me a doggie bag containing four hits of acid, four H-bombs, a gram of ketamine, two grams of marijuana, and a tiny bottle of water. I'd never felt so loved, at least not in such an organized sort of way. I emptied the entire bag into my mouth, minus the ketamine, which I split six hours later with a girl who had just lifted up her shirt to reveal a third nipple. Pierced.

Although I always laughed whenever Hal would talk about how we were the last generation of hippies, and therefore were the only people left in the country who still believed in real freedom, I still got in his Taurus every Friday. I never refused his thoughtfully packaged drugs or his friendship, really. At a rave in Hartford, I had the best sex of my life in a bathroom stall with a freshman from RISD. In Bar Harbor, while walking a loop around a bowling alley, my feet and I lost our connection. And yet, whenever I could muster the focus to look around at the half-naked fourteen-year-old girls grinding their teeth, the fat kids wearing neon ski goggles, the older men on the floor, minding their pubescent girl traps, the baby bibs, the pacifiers, the candy-stamped pills, I never saw anything more than a bunch of kids who, like me, were trying to kill themselves by stomping around in some depraved, childish dance.

AND YET, NONE of this explains why I started crying in the middle of that library. Or why my hunger, which I had been successfully ignoring since eating half of Lunch Combo 21, began mewing horribly like a run-over cat. Maybe it was the piling on of stress, maybe it was a short circuit in my nostalgic mind, or maybe it was just one of those moments that happen to me about once a year, usually while driving, when I will sob hysterically because some song comes on the radio that reminds me of my mother.

I could smell James staring over my shoulder at the screen. It was too much. I got up and jogged out the door.

As I was walking back down toward the hotel, I got a text from a 617 number. In all caps, it read:

PLEASE MEET ME AT TAXIDERMY AT 3. THIS IS ELLEN. A BIT URGENT, BUT ALSO NO BIG DEAL.

It was Performance Fleece.

BOOK THREE

w h e n he came to, Sid Finch was in what looked to be a utility closet. A bucket of sudsy water sat between his feet, which, he noticed, were bare and, somehow, scaly. On a nail above the rickety, shabbily painted white door hung his pants.

He allowed himself to look around and realized that he must have been drugged because the light from the bare bulb that hung over his head was refracting out all across the walls. Upon closer inspection, though, Finch saw that the shelves of the closet were littered with tiny mirrors, which, had Finch been a bit older or, perhaps, a bit younger, he might have recognized as pried-off bits of a disco ball. The rest of the space was completely bare save for a white Maneki Neko, who raised and lowered his paw in greeting.

FINCH HAD NO idea if he passed out again or if some part of his memory was blacked out, but when he snapped back into function, two sizable breasts swung an inch from his nose. Something warm and wet was being mushed against his forehead. Even in his scrambled state, Finch could appreciate both the lift and the heft of her breasts and the grimaceworthy perfection of the two tiny pert nipples.

He sat up, bonking his nose straight into the left breast.

The breasts swung out of sight and were replaced by a broad face and a leonine smile.

"There you are." A tinge of digital echo trailed behind each word.

Finch grunted. The girl reached down between his legs into the bucket and pulled out a sponge. She applied it to Finch's forehead. Once again, he was eye to eye with the breasts.

"You were out for a minute there. There is a reason why You Are Vivacious comes with that warning."

Finch could actually feel his brain fire the command to speak, but some greater, suffocating force kept his mouth shut. It became very obvious very quickly that he was not going to be able to say anything.

The breasts swung back up again, and he felt the sponge move to the back of his neck.

"Mona is new here. She should have asked if you had seen the allergy warning."

"Allergy?" He felt each syllable ricochet, painfully, off the broken pieces of his brain.

"Bee pollen. It's rare, but it seems you are allergic to it. Never seen anyone who was quite as allergic, though. In the past, when people have reacted badly, their eyes swell up a little and their skin goes itchy. You, well, you had a much more, let's say, intense reaction."

Finch heard the sponge plop back into the bucket, and the breasts once again were replaced by the irrefutable symmetry of her face. She peered in at his eyes and cupped his forehead with a cold, wet palm. "You have the gift to share of the most compelling eyes. Although I can't really tell what color they are. Some parts are hazel, others look green." She stood back up, dripping sponge in hand. "You are unique."

"Where?" It was all Finch could manage.

"There's nothing to worry about. When you lost consciousness, we knew what had happened, gave you the appropriate treatment, and closely monitored you. Since everything looked like it was going as we expected it to go, we didn't feel the need to get any sort of professional medical personnel involved, especially given the long history of malpractice and misdiagnosis over at San Francisco General."

The digital echo receded. Replacing it was a honeyed condescension, the sort you hear on late-night infomercials—a beautiful teenage pop star lecturing young girls on how they don't need to endure the burden of acne.

The sponge plopped back down into the bucket. He could sense Lionface stiffening a bit and regretted the violence of his thoughts. When his mother had gotten into her very own bombed-out derivative of Buddhism—a simplified, woodsier life version for white people who loved the idea of disassociation but couldn't quite get over the ugliness of the associated plastic trinkets and the *Chineseness* of it all—not much about her changed, but he did notice that the hour of required daily meditation honed both her senses and her intuition. She could better smell the booze on his breath, the marijuana smoke on his sweatshirts. She knew when he was high or if he had really gone to basketball practice. From then on, he had always felt a bit naked around anyone who might, in whatever circuitous way, subscribe to the Four Noble Truths.

Did violent thoughts emanate out farther than mundane or pleasant thoughts? Was there a different, more easily discernible tone to them? With his brain still struggling to recollect itself, Finch felt the cold bite of paranoia along the base of his spine. The water pooled at his crotch felt icy, heavy. He began to shiver.

The breasts swung down out of view again, and the face reappeared. In the same tone, which indicated that the answer to the question was an ethical matter, she asked, "Are you cold?"

"Yes." The word crept like a slug in his mouth. He shivered again.

She dipped her finger in the bucket and, coquettishly, winced. "This has gotten cold. I apologize."

"It's. Okay." Finch said. And then, "My. Pants?"

She produced a red towel and began a tousling assault on Finch's body. He felt her trained, professional touch, an efficiency to the twists and a detachment to the contact. Eyeing her breasts, which were still swinging about, he wondered if she had been a stripper.

Lionface explained, "I was a hairstylist. Before I started working here. Towel drying was always my favorite part."

Convinced now that Lionface could read his thoughts, Finch tried to blank out his brain. He tried an old technique, picturing a blue, rotating ball, but even that familiar trick, which he used in everything from sex to golf, could not quite close out the mental image of Lionface on the stripper pole. His fear dissipated into a begrudging respect—after all, who could really begrudge a beautiful woman who reads your thoughts while drying your hair?

He said, "Oh, yeah?"

"It's the only part that's not"—for the first time since she had materialized, she hesitated—"uh, that's not sharp, you know? Like, every part of styling hair is so precise, so angled. You need a protractor these days to cut bangs, and every woman wants her hair straightened first, which makes things even harder because if you screw up once, it looks like someone took a hatchet to their head. It's so nerve-racking, what with those metal scissors and the smell of burning hair and all the precision."

She lifted the towel from his hair and peered in, professionally, at his face. "I sense that I'm boring you. Here are your pants."

Looking down, he was confronted with his bulging erection. Lionface smirked, following his eyes, and said, "You have a truly abundant gift there. Your wife must be very happy."

In an attempt to force his will down to his cock, Finch frowned.

She said, "Have you ever held anything in your hands and just known it was real and that the sensation you felt from the thing wasn't just the ephemeral rush provided by words and images? Like it was a real thing?"

Finch grunted.

"I once had a pair of hiking boots like that. All-leather, none of this crappy synthetic crap, Vibram soles, and double-cushioned insides. Whenever I'd hike around the Headlands in those boots, I could feel that they were real things and not just the fluff from the assault of advertisers. Do you know what I'm talking about, Detective? The difference between the abundance of things and the false charm of words?"

Once again, he grunted.

"I can tell by the tan line on your neck that you are probably a surfer, no?"

No surfer can ever resist the opportunity to identify himself. Finch managed a nod.

"I am from San Clemente, and as a result, my brothers all surfed, and so I know a bit about it. I'm certain there are boards where you just can tell that someone put their love into shaping it and glassing it, but that there are also boards that are made entirely of fancy words and computer designs."

Finch nodded. He tried to say something, but his jaw was no longer cooperating.

"Being abundance, Detective, simply means choosing to be those real things, those real boards, those real boots, and not buying into the absurdum of adjectives and computer designs. That's all it is. It's the feeling of surfing the real board and knowing you and it are one and that those sorts of things and feelings are not rare, but are simply hidden from us by those who wish to dominate through words."

Lionface touched his shoulder. His erection jumped. Finch sat up a bit straighter. Lionface smiled and revealed a mouthful of straight, white teeth.

BY THE TIME Jim Kim pulled up in his new white Lexus, Finch's faculties had mostly returned. His legs ached and his throat felt scraped out, but he knew where he was, at least. He had no idea what had happened. All he could think was that the cyberpunks had spiked the drinks in an effort to get back at Hofspaur, but then why cause a scene? And why had Hofspaur taken him to Being Abundance? As he creakily got into Kim's car, Finch was sort of hoping that Kim would open his fat mouth and explain all.

"What the fuck happened to you, Keanu?"

"I can barely talk."

"You need to go to the hospital?"

"Probably."

"Fuck me."

"I think I'll be okay."

"The hot girl on the phone said you were allergic to pollen or something."

"How do you know?"

"That she was hot? I don't know, man, she sounded hot. You know how certain bitches just sound hot? I don't know why I have to explain these things to you when you know exactly what I'm talking about."

Finch shook his head. For a few blocks, they drove in silence. Kim turned up Franklin and started hauling up the hill toward Pacific Heights. Finch was too exhausted to ask where they were headed, so he just hung his head and stared at the floor mat.

"This bitch is acting all holy here," Kim said. It was his habit, when angry at Finch, to describe the situation to an invisible third party.

"Let's not talk about it right now."

"Okay."

"Where are we going?"

"Cleanup."

The Lexus crested California Street and barreled down toward the Marina. Although he had grown up just a few blocks from here, in a house with its own moneyed view, the sight of the hazy bay, with its clutter of sailboats and Alcatraz sitting small but significant in the center of it all, always made Finch pause and bask in an unabashed civic pride. Whenever he saw the bay or the Golden Gate Bridge swallowed up in fog, the grim-faced surfers crossing Great Highway on their way out to the shore pound at Ocean Beach, even the valley nerds wobbling along the 1 on their ridiculously efficient bicycles, he felt his hatreds soften, at least a little. It had always made sense to him that the silliest people would congregate in beautiful, inefficient spaces where they would be entertained by their surroundings but always have the built-in excuse to barely function.

THEY PULLED UP to an unremarkable two-story in the Marina. Squad cars were parked at aggressive angles out front. A female officer was spooling yellow caution tape around a chewed-up, droopy madrone.

Kim explained, "We got called here. Everyone else is out at some stupid function at the Giants game. We just have to clean up, then assign it to whoever's next up." He made eye contact with the female officer and gave her his usual salute—two hands on his belt buckle and a slight yet firm thrust of the hips. She rolled her eyes and motioned toward the front door.

THE BODY WAS in the upstairs flat—a sunny railroad-style with a kitchen whose appliances all had European names, but not quite the right European names. The floor, at least the parts not covered in blood, was an off-cordovan. The greats of American outdoor photography hung on the wall. Given those details and the location, Finch did not even really have to see the body: white, mid-twenties to early thirties, gym-built torso, probably moved to the city after college, either in the Midwest or New

England, divorced parents, house share up near Squaw Valley for the winters. Somewhere, clunking around in one of the closets, they would find a pair of skis. In the medicine cabinet, a vial of bad cocaine and a medicine bottle stuffed full of some annoyingly high-grade marijuana.

Two young, twittery officers hovered above the body. Both wore white plastic gloves. Finch and Kim exchanged a not-so-private look of disgust. Without prompting, the officers began a tandem explanation of what they thought had happened.

"We responded to the call. Landlord noticed the door was open, called up for some service issue. Toilet, I think."

"We get here, hysterical woman on the front lawn screaming in Chinese. She's pointing at the door, so we head upstairs and find the body."

"He had his ID on him?"

"Yeah, wallet with one hundred thirty-eight dollars in cash, credit cards, ID, everything. Found some marijuana paraphernalia in his pockets as well."

"What's his name?"

"William Curren. As far as we can tell, that ski pole's the murder weapon. Blood on the end of it. The size of the, uh, puncture wounds on his neck matches up with a, uh, forced entry, you know, into his throat."

Kim growled. Neither officer noticed.

"Yeah, so we did an eyeball approximation of the radius of the ski pole and approximated that the holes in his neck were a match. We scanned his, uh, parts, for traces of drugs, but there was too much, uh, obstructive blood."

Kim sighed and asked, "Anything else?"

"His fingernails."

"Yes?"

"They are clean."

The two officers went back downstairs to cordon off the block and greet the coming circus. The body was laid out on its back, arms and legs splayed out at angles that could have been produced only by a fall from over ten feet, meaning either his arms were broken or someone had purposely put him in this position. His eyes were closed, as was his mouth. Everything—face, neck, cowboy shirt, jeans, Rod Lavers—was absolutely ruined with blood.

Finch said it first. "Fuck."

"Why does he have his hands spread out like Saint Francis of Assisi?"

The usual clutter of Finch's brain cleared momentarily—he noticed, with unusual clarity, that his thoughts were moving a bit more slowly than usual. He suddenly knew what was wrong with Sarah, what he should say when he got home, but the knowing expressed itself more as a lightness in his heart rather than an actionable, worded thought. When he saw the blood—the sight of a body always was good for a little surge of adrenaline, but despite the concurrence of all this brain activity, each thought stayed separate, rational, and symmetrical—he said, "Whoever did this must have stayed with the body for a bit."

"I see six clean puncture holes all to the neck, but not much damage anywhere else. Doesn't seem to be bleeding from the head."

"Yeah, what the fuck. Where's this ski pole?"

"Over by the fridge. It's hardly bent at all."

"That's a trekking pole."

"What?"

"A trekking pole."

"What?"

"It's used for hiking, not skiing. It's a bit more rigid to support your weight as you go down hills."

"Good lord."

"How the fuck did they get these holes so clean? And why didn't this kid struggle?"

"Those *CSI*-watching retards put the wallet back in his pocket."

"Jesus."

"All right. We have William Curren, account manager at getoverit .com, office phone 4156678282, cell phone blahblahblah. Credit cards, California driver's license issued to this address, some cash, some other business cards, Caroline Sanders, associate at who cares, toothpick, no wallet photos, sandwich shop punch card . . ."

"No bloody footprints."

"Noted. No black glove."

"Anything else?"

"Fuck. Is it that time already?"

"Well, I don't think there's much else we can do here."

"All right then, let's go find the fucking Internet."

THEY WENT DOWN to Cozy's Kafe on Lombard. Kim tried to commandeer the pay-per-use Internet terminal from the woman at the desk. After five minutes of haggling, she agreed to let him use it as long as he bought two sandwiches.

William Curren had spread himself thick over the Internet. There was a Facebook account, a Myspace, a photo stream (90 percent of the photos involved outdoor activities), a Yelp account (reviews, mostly negative), and a blog entirely made up of links to eighties music videos. From his Yelp account, Kim and Finch learned Curren's last meal had been at Sun Fat, an order-by-picture Chinese dive down on Jackson Street that doubled as a Pinoy karaoke bar. He complained about the service and said his barbecue pork bun was "perfectly adequate," adding, "That's not a compliment." From Facebook, they learned that he had grown up around Boston, gone to Tufts, and moved out to the Bay Area to work for getoverit.com, which, as far as they could tell, was some sort of scam. They couldn't learn much from the comments on his wall, only that they hated his friends. After more Googling, they found his thisiswhereIbe account, a service that allowed you to "check in" wherever you went. Over the past four days, William, who seemed to go by Bill, had checked into the Secret Smoke Spot on 4th and Minna, the Blasted Shields Pub on 5th and Mission, Blue Tangerine on 18th and Valencia ("The almond cheese on the nachos is bomb."), Limon on 23rd and South Van Ness, Starbelly on Market and 16th ("service is slow, but hot!"), the 7-Eleven on Sanchez and 18th ("☺☺☺;-)"), and, finally, Sun Fat on Jackson.

Kim said, "You know what? I'm glad this kid's last meal was so shitty. You fucking white people. You go into a nice, cheap establishment where they let you get rice and chicken, hot and sour soup, and fucking egg rolls for four dollars and you complain because they won't look you in the eye? And why did he write it as a fucking haiku?"

"He put a picture of Lion-O from *ThunderCats* as his profile pic."

"Lion-O was black, don't you think?"

"Let's not do this now."

"Okay, but think about it. He was like a big black gay man."

"Jesus."

"Who the fuck is Richard Feynman, and why are all these people quoting him?"

They went on like this. Kim e-mailed some of the more pertinent info to Goldwyn back at the office. A waitress brought them their sand-wiches and wondered why two officers of the law found it necessary to speak so vulgarly.

After a few bites, Finch noticed that his thoughts had sped up a bit. But there was still the clarity, a deep blue, cold clarity. It felt strangely familiar.

"Hey, Jim."

"Yeah."

"I think I know what happened to me back in that restaurant."

With special attention paid to Lionface's breasts, Finch described what had happened at the Being Abundance Cafeteria.

Kim said, "That is fucked."

"Fucked."

"She was topless?"

"Yes. And who has ever heard of a bee pollen allergy?"

"Everything looked scaly?"

"Yeah. And some of the light was bulging."

"Your pupils do look dilated, Keanu."

"Exactly. She looked like she was checking for that."

"Are you seeing things very clearly right now? Like, is there some calm clarity to your thoughts?"

Finch burped. Kim's mouth swung slightly open, and the hard, sar-castic gleam in his eyes softened a bit. Then he picked up his knife and sawed his sandwich in half.

After chewing thoughtfully, he said, "Why would these weirdos drug a homicide detective?"

"To be fair, it might have been for the other guy."

"Do you want to go down there, arrest them all?"

"I don't know."

For a second, because neither knew what to do, they stared at the computer screen.

An e-mail popped up in Kim's in-box. It was from Goldwyn.

TO: James Kim <jkim04@sfpd.org>

FROM: Eric Goldwyn <egold@sfpd.org>

SUBJECT: getoverit.com

Thought that website looked familiar. Went back over the Dolores Stone file. Turns out her neighbor, PHILIP KIM (your cousin?), works for the same site. Called up the office. They said he hasn't been to work in nine days. Not sure if it's relevant, but thought you might be interested.

ALICE'S ADVENTURES THROUGH
THE WINDSHIELD GLASS

1. Taxidermy, the spot where I agreed to meet up with Performance Fleece, was a bar up on 22nd and Guerrero. Back when it was called The Liberties, I used to meet Adam there for drinks because none of the flabby old drunks at the bar reminded us of what we had left behind in New York. All traces of the old Irish pub had been entombed in a thick layer of staple-gunned fur—the heraldic shields that once hung above the top shelf of the bar had been replaced by Goodwill salvage stuffed animals.

Performance Fleece was at a small, furry table near the back.

She said, "Why did I want to see you?"

"Hello."

The lines on her face had fractalized, deepened. Those cheeks, which had radiated with the pink good health of New England, now looked drained of any health or protest. I admit, it made me feel a bit empowered to be on the other side of one of those girls who so tightly, and effectively, guard the secrets of their makeup bags.

Still, she smelled like freshly cut grass.

I sat down, smiling stupidly. She clacked the salt and pepper shakers together. Pewter deer heads. I asked, "What are you drinking?"

She shook her head, but then, miraculously, smiled. She said, "Whiskey and soda."

I went up to the bar and ordered two. The bartender looked me over and poured two doubles.

We drank them down without saying much. The color—that good post–hockey practice color—flushed back into her face.

"So," I said, "what's this about?"

"I'm a direct person."

"Yeah."

"So, I'll just come out and say it, okay?"

"Sure."

"I left Mel."

2. There's no need to detail a girl's domestic misery in her own words, especially when those words are frazzled words, so for Performance Fleece's sake, I'll paraphrase. She and Mel had been having problems for quite some time. They had met as freshmen at Williams—he, the dark Italian star of the hockey team (her words), and she, the blue-blood field hockey star from *Choate* (her italics). Their relationship had taken on easy contours from the start. In a nice private-school way, she and Mel were well aligned and stayed so for years.

Whenever she felt bored, she'd ask Mel to take her down to visit his family in Providence. There, she would sit down at one of those Italian feasts they show in those movies, with gigantic *happy* women (her words) who wore gold jewelry and drove American cars and men who smelled like trashy women. It was Mel's family, more than Mel himself, that kept Performance Fleece around. She had always shown an interest in other cultures. (I snickered at this, but after she stabbed me in the back of the hand with a cocktail straw, I shut up.) *No*, not lame, like *that*. Not like those girls who travel abroad to *Tibet* or some fucked-up place and take 16-mm photos of poor children playing *soccer*, but more like I was interested in *fucking* a lot of different types of guys, like in middle school, I gave one of the METCO kids a blowjob after he got done with football practice. At Choate, I stole out of my dorm and let two of the Mexican guys who worked in the dining hall fondle and suck on my breasts, for like an hour, and rub me. Over the pants. (Again, her words. Note: longest sentence I had heard out of her. Plus, she giggled.)

She did not know why she stayed with Mel for all those years. Maybe the stability of the logic behind their union helped her with the guilt she felt over her true inner slut. Or maybe she did love his family enough to lease out their son. Maybe Boston just didn't make sense to her without Mel. They had the same friends, they ate at the same five restaurants, they drank at the same two bars, they shopped at the same supermarket, and both took the T to Downtown Crossing. Love and cities are always inextricably entwined. There's no restaurant or corner store or run-down dive in any city that doesn't double as a monument for a lost love. I think that's why we always stop and stare whenever we come across a girl crying in public. We sense the imprint of a memory being pressed onto the sidewalk, onto the building contours, onto the names of the streets.

Boston, Performance Fleece explained, had become just a photo reel of her years with Mel. In the first frame, she and Mel move her mom's old furniture into the bottom floor of a run-down duplex in Cambridgeport. Farther along the reel, after having lived all over Boston, they stand smiling next to a SOLD sign. She had just accepted the progression of these images, just as she had accepted Choate, lacrosse camp, Williams, and, ultimately, Mel. Then, one day, for reasons unknown, she simply didn't. Everything became ugly to her—the hats the cashiers at Dunkin' Donuts had to wear, the grease on the handgrips on the T, the excess butter served with the bread at Bertucci's, the endless talk about the Red Sox, the droves of pale, mute Chinese kids, forever shuttling on the Red Line between Kendall/MIT and Harvard Square, the green everywhere on Saint Patrick's Day and the kids who never took an interest in anything other than Tom Brady suddenly asking one another what part of Ireland their people were from, the constant questions from their married friends about when they were going to "repay the party," the drabness of the drive on the 2 up to her parents' house in Beverly, the only stretch of road in America where the trees are bare year-round, the bartender at their neighborhood bar, a guy Mel described as "the salt of the earth," and his stupid philosophy about what constituted "honest work," mostly stolen from *Good Will Hunting*.

When they left Boston for San Francisco, the scaffolding of their love fell away. She had known this would happen. The move was her idea. She had gotten a job offer at Wells Fargo and found him a position at a start-up. She reasoned that they would never get to live in California ever again, and he couldn't think of much of a rebuttal. His best friend from college lived in San Francisco, and he was tapped into a network of good dudes. They'd moved into the condo on Natoma Street nine months ago.

Last night, she told Mel about her latest affair. She didn't understand the timing, herself, but it had something to do with her feelings toward me. Or maybe it didn't. She didn't really know. Either way, Mel had responded badly to the news. He had assumed that their move to California was, at least in some way, an effort to salvage what was left. He had said some things she had expected him to say and one thing she had not.

She had spent the night at a twenty-four-hour Starbucks in Laurel Village before deciding to text me.

3. By the time she finished, we were both drunk. I had forgotten about the Advanced Creative Writer. Or, perhaps, I should say, I had misplaced my panic. We talked about baseball. She, like all sturdy girls from Boston, knew just enough about the Red Sox to carry on a conversation, but not enough to raise concern.

But then she asked, "Did you call that detective?" and I remembered that we were in grave danger. She must have seen the alarm on my face because she asked, "What happened?"

I told her. Or at least, I told her most of it. I left out the second hottest girl at the bar. She listened quietly, but as I kept filling in details, her face slowly caved in. When I finished telling her about being attacked, she whispered, "Fuck this."

"Yeah."

"So the kid in the van."

"Yes."

"He saw me, too."

"He doesn't know who you are, though. You're not friends with his creative writing teacher."

"Still, he probably knows where I live. Lived."

"Maybe."

"Are you safe?"

"Who knows?"

"Well, if they had wanted to kill you, wouldn't they have just killed you when they attacked you?"

I had not considered this. It was a bit embarrassing to admit, so I just nodded. She continued, "Maybe they're trying to send you a message or something. Or maybe this is just a fucked-up coincidence."

"How could it be a coincidence?"

"These things, they usually end up being a coincidence."

"Okay, but let's pretend it's not a coincidence. What is it, then?"

We talked like this for a while. I grew mildly annoyed, not by Performance Fleece, but more with myself for my inability to create a plausible scenario. Everything sounded crazy, paranoid. I blamed my career as a fiction writer, but Performance Fleece noted that if I were actually anything of a fiction writer, I could have thought up some version of things where we both would be safe. Plus, she added, you don't get to claim that you're a writer until someone has paid you to publish something.

It sounded about right.

4. That afternoon, Performance Fleece showed up at the Hotel St. Francis with three plastic tubs. This is what was inside.

Tub one: two sets of fitted sheets (dark brown and crimson, queen, flannel), a down comforter with a crocheted duvet (stuffed full, fruit orchard in fall), a Hudson's Bay blanket, an Afghan throw, a business calculator, two business suits (gray, black), a tangle of nylons, a rubber bath mat, a Tempur-Pedic pillow, an architecturally advanced desk lamp, a can of Ajax, a bottle of mineral oil, a pack of tarot cards, a Bose Wave radio, a field hockey stick, three pairs of shin guards.

Tub two: a paper bag filled with hair bands, two pairs of jeans (one weathered, one black, both sculpted and rigid), black pumice, a small plastic container, which, upon further investigation, held both a mouth guard *and* a retainer, a camping headlamp, a propane canister, a white bathrobe, two plush white towels, a Brillo pad and one of those yellow and green sponges, a puffy jacket, a peacoat, two cashmere sweaters, all manner of underwear, and her two newest purchases: a thirty-two-inch Louisville Slugger and a four-inch hunting knife.

Resting on top of tub two was a dehumidifier.

I get congested easily, she explained.

I admit it. Some of the happiest memories of my life are of waking up in some girl's dorm room and inhaling the synthesis of dirty, sweaty clothes, scented candles, burned hair, microwaved popcorn, and Secret. In college, whenever I found myself in this Byzantium of white girliness, I'd always sneak off to take a shower, where a patch of brightly colored hair and body products sprouted on the scummy tile floor. On the shower head, loofahs hung heavy-headed, like slightly browned iris blossoms. I'd always take my time and lather myself with every gel, every goo, every mall-bought, industrially scented, animal-tested product that would never have been allowed in my childhood home. Once, after drunkenly pawing at a heavy freshman who had been impressed by a story I had written in the school's literary magazine, I bounded in the morning to her shower to wash off the congealed cheese from the half-eaten pizza I had passed out on, only to find a relic from my childhood spoiling the usual bouquet of loofahs—a red, corrosive, nasty washcloth that I immediately knew belonged to the freshman's Korean roommate. It was enough to send me home without a shower. Since then, I've felt some shame over these sorts of things (we don't have to talk about it, really), but within the vault of my sense memories, no collection of smells quite perks me up like the smells that live in the shared dormitory bathrooms of the elite colleges of the Northeast.

So when Performance Fleece opened up the third tub and began stacking up her collection of moisturizers, conditioners, and shaving products, I fell halfway in love.

5.   We had sex on top of the crocheted orchard duvet, but the desperation of our earlier go had dissipated. I kept slipping out and apologizing. She demanded we try at a slower pace. I responded to this emasculation by trying to jam my finger up her ass. It worked, sort of, but then it really didn't work. Given the state in which we had found each other again, I didn't understand what might be wrong. Maybe it was, let's say, our modest surroundings, but Performance Fleece, true-blue New

Englander, had kept her silence about the mattress, the ramps of dust left in the corners by the cleaning girl, the black veins spreading across the bathtub, the rust and the scum on the faucet, the smell of retread and hard-burned cooking oil, the ominous thuds against the wall, all of which were too soft to be anything but a body. Her only commentary on the room was to note that the pastoral print that hung over the bed had been painted by someone in the Hudson River School, but she couldn't quite remember the name of the artist. She didn't comment on how the print had been tacked to the wall without a frame or that it had been blackened so badly by smoke that it now looked more like a Bosch.

Is there anything more attractive to an unsettled man than a woman who silently endures it all? I rolled over, and we did it again. This time, I think I was better.

She went off to the shower. I lay back and waited for the gusts of steam, carrying the heavy scent of products, to waft into the room. For the first time in what seemed like days, I thought about the Baby Molester and the night she showed up at my door, half naked and drunk, asking for a cigarette. It felt like years ago. All the associated panic—the beating, the cryptic threats, the black masks, the blue Astro van—now felt abstracted from my endless list of concerns, as if it had all been part of a story for which I was no longer being held responsible.

I'm hopeless like that. Find me a girl, and I forget the rest of my life happened.

Content, waiting for Performance Fleece to reemerge, I picked up my phone and went back over my browsing history.

THE DIGNITY PROJECT

WILLIAM THOMAS CURREN

B: DECEMBER 18 1984. GLENVIEW, ILLINOIS

D: MAY 12 2009. SAN FRANCISCO, CA

William Curren, known as Bill to his friends and colleagues, was born at the Northwestern Memorial Hospital in Chicago, Illinois, on December 18, 1984, the first and only son of Stacy and Michael Curren. He spent much of his childhood in a two-story colonial with black shutters. At least one summer of his youth was spent playing Little League baseball. From a young age, Mr. Curren displayed a high academic aptitude, placing in the 95th percentile and above on all of his yearly statewide assessment tests. He carried this academic aptitude to high school, where he finished in the top 20 percent of his class. His academic strengths and his success as a debater gained him acceptance into Tufts University, where Mr. Curren became heavily involved in the Beelzebubs, the college's acclaimed a cappella group.

After a successful academic career at Tufts, Mr. Curren graduated with a 3.45 GPA while double-majoring in political science and economics. He spent the summer after graduation at Wrightsville Beach in North Carolina, where, according to our sources, he tended bar and enjoyed the local nightlife. In February 2007, Mr. Curren flew out to San Francisco to interview at getoverit .com, then a start-up company. He moved into a house share on California and Broderick before finding his own apartment at 236 Jackson Street in the city's Marina District. According to his friends,

Mr. Curren enjoyed the vibrancy of the city and lived every second
like it was his last.

I stopped reading there. Performance Fleece walked out of the bathroom, mummified in terry cloth. When she saw my face, she dropped
her plastic shower caddy. A pink can of shaving cream went clattering
across the floor.

BOOK FOUR

when Kim dropped Finch off at his car, still parked
a block away from the Porn Palace, Finch restrained himself from grabbing at any of the thoughts that floated by in slow, eddying circles.
Despite his best push for sanity, a physical reflex that made his sphincter
contract, these thoughts appeared to him as catfish swimming slowly at
the bottom of a clear blue lagoon. Every once in a while, one of the fish
would pop to the surface and say something. One said, "Sarah only loves
you because she feels obligated, but she's also the sort of girl who feels
better under obligation." Another said, "Visit your mother. She was trying her best." Another said, "Visit your father. He was trying his best."
Another said, "That poor kid was stabbed to death by a ski pole. How

many times in Tahoe were you lucky?" Another sang, "Going to leave this broke-down paaa-lace/on my hands/*and* my knees/I will *roll-roll-roll*/Make myself a bed by the waterrrrr-*side*/in my time/in my time/I will *roll-roll-roll*."

Finch closed his eyes. Through his eyelids, he could see the outlines of the fish swimming about in a reddish miasma of partial images, muted light, blood, and words. For some reason, it was clear that he could not catch these fish, or throw them out of his mind. And although he knew from experience that the psilocybin had passed the stage where a visual hallucination was anything more than a shadow, he could feel their unusual boniness, their prehistoric architecture.

What to do? He drove home, picked up his board and his wet suit, and drove to the beach.

SID "KEANU" FINCH had started surfing because of *Point Break*, but he kept surfing because the ritual of suiting up in the parking lot, the daily baptism in freezing water, the panic of being dumped, the rush of the drop, and the preening satisfaction of the ride atomized his daily mind into unrecognizably small, disparate parts. While floating in the lineup, thoughts like, "Where is my career going?" would circulate through his head, but once a wave welled up in front of him and the demands of the sport presented themselves, all those nagging concerns lost their immediacy. His fellow locals were all after similar annihilation. Some were methheads incapable of hacking it down in Santa Cruz. Others were jaded LA kids who had made the pilgrimage up north to this Mecca of oldish, charmish Edwardians, pale girls, and the strict, protective business zoning laws that kept out Applebee's and their ilk. A smaller proportion were like Finch—San Francisco natives who surfed OB because its riptides, deadly closeouts, sharks, blooms of fecal coliform bacteria, and general gnarliness made it the only place in the city where one could escape from the totality of yuppie things.

Finch drove down Geary past Land's End and the Sutro Baths, past the curve at the Cliff House, and around Seal Rock, between whose craggy double humps he had once been stranded, surrounded by five hundred indifferent seagulls, after a rogue wave snapped his leash. The catfish in his brain, perhaps noticing his distraction, chirped up more insistently: "Stabbed to death with a ski pole! Yes, the cradle of love . . . don't rock easy, it's true. . . . There is no difference between you and Kim anymore, he has taken on your hate, you, his bitterness. There's a million ways to be, you know that there are. You know that there are. . . ."

But as he wound down the hill toward Kelly's Cove, he could see that the winds were straight offshore and that the waves were about head-high, maybe 1.5× on the sets.

No school of catfish, or their words of wisdom, can hold a surfer's mind hostage when he sees perfect conditions and an empty lineup.

IN THE PARKING lot at Sloat, a little militia of surfers were standing behind their trucks, each one in some stage of disrobing. Finch recognized Doc Samson, an OB local who had come to surf celebrity when a national magazine published a feature that revealed, in anthropological detail, the oddity of a man who surfed *and* practiced medicine. The good doctor was accompanied, as always, by his surf buddy Chris Isaak, whose "Wicked Game" video occupied a monolithic space in Finch's history of masturbation.

When Finch got out of his car, he heard raised voices. Two men, stripped to the waist, were shouting at each other. One of them had his phone in his still-wet hand.

"Fuck you!"

"Fuck you!"

"Fuck you!"

"Why don't you get your fucking kook friends down here so you can all have a fucking faggot gang bang on the beach? Where the fuck are you from, anyway? I've surfed here for twenty-six years and I've never seen your ugly ass before."

"I've lived in the Sunset for eight years, motherfucker."

"I'm going to break that fucking phone."

Finch walked over to Chris Isaak and asked what was going on. Isaak had just started struggling out of his wet suit, and as he began peeling the rubber off his chest, Finch felt a vague, nostalgic shame.

It was the oldest running joke at the beach. Isaak gave everyone a hard-on because they couldn't look at his gorgeous face without imagining Helena Christensen and all those tits and mascara.

How many socks had been irreparably stiffened, how many boxes of Kleenex had been emptied to catch all the semen wasted on account of that video?

"How was it out there?" Finch asked.

"Holy shit."

"That's what it looks like."

"Hit up that left down past the Cliffs of Despair. Barrels all day."

"What's up with those two dudes?"

"Stokereporter."

"Ah. Fuck him, then."

Stokereport was an MMS/user-generated website providing surf reports for the breaks from Bolinas down to Capitola's Wild Hook. The posters on the site referred to themselves as "Stokereporters," and were mostly kooks—out-of-towners who cluttered lineups with whoops, clumsy takeoffs, bleach-blond hair, noodle arms, lame cutbacks, and brightly colored, criminally overpriced longboards.

Old salty locals, who either lived by the beach or hawked over updated geological survey maps and wind pattern trackers to guess at the conditions, regarded Stokereporters with a gentrifical venom. Stokereporters were blamed for overcrowded conditions, unfavorable winds, broken boards, drop-ins, and beach pollution. When the Coast Guard had to rescue four different surfers in the span of six days during a massive northwest swell, it was discovered that three of the men were Stokereporters who had read about the perfect big-wave conditions and had paddled out. These incidents escalated the conflict between locals and Stokereporters. Both sides found access to the familiar linguistic arsenal of right versus left, life versus death, and the military. It had all come to a head at the Riptide Bar up on Judah, when a Stokereport get-together was crashed by a group of drunk old locals, including the infamous Bad Vibes Bob, who had shown up with a riding crop. No one was arrested, largely thanks to Finch, but the resulting brawl sent one Stokereporter to the hospital.

Down at the end of the parking lot, the local had managed to wrest away the Stokereporter's phone and was threatening to smash it against the ground.

Finch laughed. Chris Isaak laughed, too.

FINCH SUITED UP and paddled out to the spot Chris Isaak had mentioned. It took only one steep, barreling left to forget about William "Bill" Curren, Being Abundance, psilocybin, Hofspaur, Dolores Stone, Sarah's distance, the swinging breasts, Kim's stupor, and the bony persistence of the prehistoric catfish. As he paddled back out, he saw Bad Vibes Bob's red board tombstoning out of the break and then, a second later, Bad Vibes Bob's gray head popping up out of the surf.

A calm, quite different from the mushroom clarity, washed over Finch. The winds were cooperating, the waves were peeling perfectly, and all the bros were out.

On his third thumping, overhead left of the session (Finch had a habit, probably born out of his childhood fascination with baseball stats, of counting his rides and categorizing them by the direction, shape, and length), a shoulder hopper dropped in on him, lost his balance, and tumbled headfirst into the trough. Finch heard the crunch as his fins ran over the offender's board and was launched into the white water. As the washing machine gathered him up, he could feel the shoulder hopper struggling to get to the surface. In an effort to separate their bodies before the churn sent them both back over the falls, Finch pushed himself away and curled himself up into a ball and began his routine of counting slowly in his head to dispel the panic. He felt the surge of water catch his body, and, in a sledgehammer's arc, he was slammed, shoulder-first, onto the ocean floor. Sixteen seconds later, his leash went slack.

At the surface, a red-faced, scraggly bottle blond was gasping for air. A few feet down the beach floated the sawed-off remains of a

Coke-bottle-green Harbour Noserider. He recognized the man from a poster someone had put up at the Riptide Bar, which had photos of all the Stokereporters, descriptions of their boards, and a simple declaration: WANTED: FOR POSEURISM.

"Bro, look what you did to my fucking board!"

"You dropped in on *me*, asshole. I should be yelling at you for nicking up my fins."

"That's a sixteen-hundred-dollar board, asshole. You fucking ran me right over."

A second wave, hollow and frothy, crashed on their heads. Finch went back over the falls, bounced on the sand, started up the slow count.

"Fucking shit, man. If someone walks out in front your car, do you just run them over? Where is your fucking discretion?"

"Post something about it on your website, bro."

His contrarian nature and soft voice absolved Finch from the usual charges of cop bullying. There had been a short stretch, right after graduating from the academy, when he had picked up a whiff of menace in his dealings with wealthy women. In particular, there was an instance when, while pacing around the maid's quarters of a mansion up on Pacific, he had purposely knocked over and shattered a Ming vase—a *good* Ming—owned by a woman whose fifteen-year-old son had just stolen her car. Although his old patrol habit of pulling over cars with NPR bumper stickers might be interpreted as abuse by those who caught the tickets for going 46 in a 35, every cop he knew had to keep at least one good joke going. But aside from those two quirks, which he attributed directly to unresolved mom issues, Sid Finch sought out the losing side of any confrontation. He was always kind to fat women. He felt sentimental over the poor terrorists in Iraq who, holding an AK-47 for the first time in their lives, were cut down by American bullets. He hadn't voted in the last election because he couldn't fight how sorry he felt for soggy old John McCain. After his childhood love of the Giants had been annihilated by Barry Bonds's arrogance, he had even rejected the idea of rooting for a team, choosing instead to hope only for the humiliation of the Yankees and, in time, the Red Sox.

While the rest of the judging world might choose a side based on silly, affected opinions, Finch's choice came on a more visceral level. In any conflict, one side was going to get killed. He would forever be fighting for that side. In San Francisco, that meant being police.

Finch agreed that the Stokereporters were surf-ethically wrong, but he had long since determined—despite their use of technology, their superior numbers, and their cloying enthusiasm—these limp-armed poseurs were, in fact, the underdog. Finch could understand why his fellow locals had fashioned the battle as a Thermopylae, with the buff, salty cast of locals fighting valiantly against the hordes of offending kooks, but whenever he saw a Stokereporter flailing, panicked, whenever he read one of their posted narratives, riddled with nuanced self-congratulation about trying to paddle past the break on a 2OH OB day, whenever some pale, concave-chested kid covered in body acne walked up to him in the parking lot and asked for help with his wet suit zipper, Finch knew the Thermopylae comparison was wrong.

When he grabbed a fistful of the Stokereporter's poseur-blond scraggle, nobody was more surprised than Finch. A wave welled up, the face going from green to gunmetal gray as the water shifted away from the sun. The dredge kicked up, and, as both men were being sucked back, Finch watched with detachment as the man's eyelids peeled back. As the lip detonated on their heads, Finch found himself simply appreciating the aesthetic magnitude of the man's terror.

He kept his grip through the tumble and through the fourteen-second washing machine. When the wave let up, he saw the man's squarish, capped teeth inside his gaping mouth, the equine flare of his nostrils. Nausea crept up from the pit of Finch's stomach. He let go.

The Stokereporter had a few things to say, but it was just theater, the chronically insecure man's version of a spank bank.

THE STOKEREPORTER TOOK the next wave in. Finch paddled back out past the break. Floating three hundred yards from the beach, he tried to summon up some reasoning behind the attack.

The ocean went slack. The wind picked up from the south. Down the beach, he could see about a dozen guys floating around on the gray water. He could hear them yammering on about the credibility of some shark encounter down in Montara. The nausea subsided. Bad Vibes Bob paddled over and asked him what had happened. Finch shook his head. Bad Vibes Bob said, "Fuck them, right?"

Finch nodded, stared down south, where the parking lot gave way to the cliffs of Fort Funston. When the Porn Palace had closed, they had moved the munitions down here, and when Fort Funston closed, they hauled the guns up to the Marina. He thought it might mean something, but again, he couldn't quite figure out what.

Fuck it, he thought, and paddled back to the beach.

AS HE TROD up the hill that led from the edge of the water to the parking lot, Finch saw the Stokereporter and four other men standing behind his car. Both pieces of the man's broken board were laid out on Finch's hood. The nausea returned. Finch closed his eyes and saw the white flash of one of the catfish's protruding bones.

Finch made a mental note: Get to the hospital.

The Stokereporters advanced uneasily across the parking lot. Finch quickly checked around, but everyone else was in the water or had gone home.

"Looking around for your buddies?"

One of the catfish whispered, "Feel the color of his voice. Insubstantial. He's still broken. Think of the odds you're at now."

Finch gave in. The fish were right. The Stokereporter, flanked by his friends, stalked right up to Finch and said, "You're lucky I don't call the fucking cops on you, man."

Finch punched him straight in the forehead. The Stokereporter's eyes rolled back in his head. He staggered into the arms of one of his buddies. Clearly, all of them had been expecting the usual routine: screaming, occasional shoving, homophobic epithets, and empty threats.

He laughed. The catfish all surfaced. They laughed, too.

What else to do? Finch pushed past, tossed the broken board over the cliff.

After yelling a bit, the Stokereporters scattered. Two hopped on down the cliff to retrieve the remains of the board. Another helped his concussed friend find a seat on the bumper of his truck. The last one pulled out his phone, and, from the way his fingers were moving

on the screen, looked to be looking something up. No one looked at
Finch.

No matter, thought Finch.

FINCH DIDN'T QUITE know what to make of anything yet and
had already forgotten his mental note to go to the hospital, so he peeled
out of the parking lot at Sloat and headed south. He had always loved
driving down the 1 past Pacifica through Devil's Slide, especially in the
fall, when the furrowed fields around Half Moon Bay sagged with their
heavy, orange fruit. The uselessness of everything that grew down the 1
had appealed to him as a kid: the pumpkins, the kiwi farms, the trust
fund projects with their silly, reassuring crops: pie fillings, star fruit,
Brussels sprouts. His junior year in high school, he had lain down with
Loretta Neill in a pumpkin patch down near the Princeton Jetty. Staring
up at the array of stars, Finch gave what amounted to a spoken word
performance of Townes Van Zandt's "Loretta," a song he had picked almost entirely out of the great coincidence that there was a song with the
same name as his girlfriend. He could still remember each word, just as
he could still remember the startling pungent smell on his fingers, the
bumping of teeth, the chirp of his own brain celebrating the start of
something new. Hundreds of pumpkins, swollen, moonlit, stood sentry
as Finch and Loretta squirmed and pushed and then wallowed a bit in
the cocoons of their guilt. Afterward, they lay on their backs and he
explained why Townes Van Zandt was a real singer and Johnny Cash,
whom she loved, was just a charming impostor. He was always ruining
these moments with his awkwardly timed vitriol. He honestly thought
Loretta's life would be improved if she upgraded from Johnny Cash to

Townes, just as he honestly believed that his teachers would be better off dead, or that his parents would be better off if they took acid at least once a month and smoked weed every day. Loretta, he remembered, had said that Townes was ugly, and a misogynist, to boot. All his women were kindly whores or wives with impossibly warm hearts. Everyone was always leaving. Even Loretta, she explained, is a carousing bartender whom Townes only likes because he can have her any time. Finch had nothing to say. She huddled deeper into his houndstooth coat and sighed. He squeezed her fingers and felt happy anticipating the rest of the night: the planned stop-in at the Denny's in Pacifica, her flushed cheeks, unraveling hair, the wordless car ride back home, both of them listening to Guy Clark, the median between Townes and Johnny Cash, on the tinny speakers of his mother's beat-up Mercedes. Back then, at the height of their young love, Finch, who had never bent in anything, imagined the hundreds of compromises he could make for Loretta.

Through the pastel sameness of Daly City's row houses, old Finch's mind stayed on Loretta, who had died at nineteen of meningitis. Loretta! Her chicken legs, her tuft of dry, pale yellow hair, her asymmetrical eyebrows, the persistence of her wool, earflapped ski caps, the way she kept both hands on her forty when she drank.

For the first time in years, Finch began to cry. Softly, and to himself.

Hurtling down the hill now toward Pacifica on the 1, where you can see the ocean fan out from Fort Funston all the way down to Pillar Point, he rooted one of his Townes Van Zandt CDs out of the glove box and sang, chokingly, along.

He realized how long it had been since he had sung along to anything. Something has gone wrong, he thought, and felt embarrassed at the clumsiness of the declaration. Something has been wrong for years.

He closed his eyes, searching for the fish, expecting to see their tails flailing as they burrowed their bony heads further into his brain, but he only found the dry, vacuous space of his mind.

Litost. The torment that arises when we unexpectedly encounter our own expansive misery. It had been Loretta's favorite word, borrowed from her favorite book written by her favorite author. Finch had taken her to task on Kundera—if she shunned Townes for his misogyny, why accept a lecherous old Czech? All of Kundera's women, he pointed out, were whores, glorified courtesans, or, even worse, philosophical and political symbols. At least Townes cared about his whores. She had answered, simply, that she chose Kundera because he, above all other writers, understood what it meant to be in love.

It was too much. Johnny Cash, ski hats, and *Kundera.* He began to be mean to her.

His memories of that period in his life were so foreign to him now that they seemed almost to belong to someone else, someone whom he might now despise. How had he, who no longer read or listened to music, been the sort of person who could muster the arrogance, and the care, to categorically dismiss Johnny Cash, or, for God's sake, Milan Kundera? And while the rationalist in him, the trained detective who could trace back circumstance into motive, could posit an explanation of how the fire of his young love had been extinguished at Loretta's death—none of us really ever fall out of love with the first woman who agrees to return us the favor—he could not recognize the totality of that younger self who had sat entranced by all that had provided kindling for that little blaze.

He understood how he had gotten so old. But how had he ever been so young?

THE BUZZING OF his phone interrupted his reverie. It was Kim. He sent him to voice mail.

THERE WERE STILL things that could shift him around—Opening Day, walking past the tunnel at Pac Bell Park to take in the Giants in their papal whites, tossing around warm-ups; the letter and family photos he received every September from his childhood pen pal, Mishka, who had emigrated from Russia and was now a computer programmer in Atlanta; the perfectly conical dunes of spices his mother piled up, for God knew what reason, on the kitchen counter every Thanksgiving; the uncontrollable, childish grins that broke out across the faces of his scowling, salty friends whenever they pulled out a barrel and knew that someone else had witnessed it; how the lotion-obsessed Chinese women of Clement Street hawkishly guarded their trays of dumplings; the busted gait of the dogs that trailed around after the ratty, homeless kids on Haight Street; and here, eating a heavy, glazed scone in his car, outside of a bakery in Pescadero, thinking, for the first time in years, about Johnny Cash, Townes, pumpkins, *litost*, ski hats, Olde English, and a dead girl.

Something buried in Finch's heart picked up its birdy head, shook off a generation of dust, and floated around aimlessly. He felt the sort of joy only Tolstoy could ever describe, the sort of joy that the younger Finch, sharp, modern fellow that he was, had always hated Tolstoy for acknowledging. For a second, probably more, he was ecstatically happy. And then, when he could take it no more, he took his phone out of his pocket and checked his messages.

THERE WERE FOUR. The first three were from Kim. Dolores Stone's neighbor had disappeared. Goldwyn and Kim were going for drinks at Irene's at seven, if he wanted to come. The *Chronicle* had already left eighteen phone calls at the office about the Stone murder. The last message had been sent from an unfamiliar number. A woman's voice said, "Hello, Officer. I know this will upset you, but when you were resting at the restaurant, I took the liberty of calling my phone from your phone, you know, so I would know your number. I imagine it has been a bit of a strange day for you. If you would like an explanation, please call me at this number."

What did Lionface want? He called the number and got a nonpersonalized voice mail. Seconds later, he received a text:

218A 39th Avenue. x-street: Fulton. Will be here till 9 PM. Plz call when your nearby.

P IS FOR PSYCHO

1. The detective who picked up the phone identified himself as Jim Kim. I tried to not be bowled over by this. Every Korean is named Kim, and no Kim has ever done me a favor. This Kim told us to meet him at the Starbucks on 20th and Mission. He would be wearing a Wisconsin sweatshirt.

We called a cab.

My panic internalized. My cheeks and hips ached. Ellen, hunched over and huddled in her performance fleece, deflated, slowly.

We, Ellen and I, said some things about how the cops would help.

The cab company called and said the driver was downstairs. We told him to meet us in an alley behind the Hotel St. Francis, and, with the promise of a decent tip for the trip of five blocks, told him to drive us, circuitously, to Starbucks.

He laughed.

The shame was a welcome intrusion from the terror. I whispered, not quite into Ellen's ear, but more into her neck: Everything is going to be all right.

WE FOUND JIM Kim near the back at a round table, one of those pieces of furniture birthed completely out of corporate research, in which you can see the honed edge of market math, but cannot figure out how to put two separate cups of coffee on it. The Wisconsin sweatshirt was tied around his shoulders. Kim, anticipating our arrival, I guess, had taken the liberty of pulling up two empty chairs. I tried to smile at him. He scowled.

I consoled myself with his remarkable ugliness. His head, as my mother might have said, looked like a filthy little potato.

He asked, "Any problem finding the place?"

"What?"

"I was kidding. It's Starbucks."

I already hated him, but I apologized for myself.

He asked, "Do you know what this place used to be like before you people started moving into this neighborhood? It wasn't a *Starbucks*, I'll tell you that."

"Sorry."

"How can you be sorry? You don't even know what I'm talking about."

Ellen, finally, sat down. I resisted the urge to sit in her lap.

She asked, "Can you please tell us what's going on?"

Again, the eyebrows rose up. He grimaced. "That's what I ask you, darling."

"Well, we have no idea."

"Is this your boyfriend?" Without bothering to look at me, he pointed a stubby, yellow finger in my face.

"Yes."

2. I would like to try to explain my happiness.

First, let me concede the very real distance between the fear of my impending death and the discovery of love. That is quite the pendulum. And, if we accept, for reason's sake, a spatial map of our happiness, where the far left side represents a game-winning hit in a Little League game or the birth of a child, and the far right side represents the death of a parent, or parents, or, say, the realization that, despite being decent-looking and interesting enough, less good-looking and less interesting white guys will have a better crack at all the pretty blond girls of the world, or, when at wit's end, you realize that you cannot really pick up and move to Prague, the Yukon, or Des Moines, Iowa, even, without amplifying your awareness of your otherness; if we evaluate happiness the same way we evaluate, say, baseball statistics (I'm not arguing this is a bad method, by the way), where the best we ever hit is .300 (Sabermetrics, if you only knew how badly you have ruined our failure-based metaphors! Should I say, instead, the best we ever OBP is .440?), I can also concede that when you, in a matter of minutes, go from fearing your grisly end to hearing that you are someone's boyfriend, even if you don't really *know* the girl, even if she's agreeing just to speed along a conversation or misdirect an asshole detective, well, then, I concede, under duress, that all I felt was the breeze of the swing.

But the only evidence I've ever found of a compassionate God is how he allows us to excerpt our happiest memories up out of their contexts and hold them with the same care Saint Francis of Assisi holds up his little animals. I can remember passing around a joint in an orange Volvo with my three best friends, listening, in reverential silence, to *Enter the Wu-Tang*. After "Protect Ya Neck," we plodded through a stoned debate over who was the better leadoff hitter: Rickey Henderson or Inspectah Deck. My friends were all Jews, who were working through their own psychodrama of strangeness. There's no doubt that we were "cultural tourists," and while we might have occasionally *felt* the song, our devotion came more from the spike of confidence that comes with rapping bluntedly along: "I'm more rugged than slave man boots. New recruits, I'm fucking MC troops. I break loops, and trample shit when I stomp!" And even though it's hard to fault three Jews and an Asian in North Carolina for using hip-hop to hack out four little black doppelgangsters, it's now quite passé to write, at least this earnestly, about how those sessions in the car were among the happiest moments of my life.

So. Even though I didn't know what would eventually happen between us, when I heard Ellen confirm that I was, indeed, her boyfriend, my head glowed with the heat of a thing being alchemized.

I wonder if there has ever been a more equivocal explanation of happiness. But, it's the best you'll get out of this man who has always hit well below the Mendoza Line.

3.   "So you saw William Curren last Thursday."

"Yes."

"You went to the Uptown with three girls, after which you were attacked."

"Yes."

"Was Ms. Ellen one of these girls?"

"No, I wasn't."

"I only talked to one of the girls."

"Can you describe her?"

"I would describe her as unattractive. Unathletic body."

"I know that you and Mr. Curren liked to smoke weed together at work. Was Mr. Curren involved in any drug trafficking activity?"

"What? How do you know that?"

"Please just answer the questions."

"Hold on. . . . Let me check something on my phone."

"I am a detective. This is serious."

"Holy shit, you guys use Facebook?"

"Philip, try to focus. Do you have an explanation as to what happened here?"

"These things are usually coincidence?"

"Look at him. What could he kill?"

"Please let him answer the questions."

"Uh, can we talk about the message?"

"Ma'am, would you mind stepping outside, or at least going up to the counter for a second? I have a Korean thing to discuss with your boyfriend."

"I have a right to be present for an interrogation."

"That is not a right."

"We want a lawyer."

"This is not an interrogation or even a questioning. Neither of you is a suspect. You have no need for a lawyer."

"I'm staying."

"Whatever."

"Okay."

"Can you please take a look at this, Philip? Do you recognize who might have written it?"

Dear Philip,

It's been four days since Sue perished in that tragic accident. John, my son, has gotten deteriorated. His anger is stultifying. Yesterday, he tells me he is going to shove a remote control up my ass. I am afraid that my wife's death pushed him over into dark, desecrated anger. Before, I thought he was just a rambunctious pubescent boy. But since his mother's death, he has been lashing out and throwing things at me and his sister. This morning, I saw him in the shed and he was eyeing my chainsaw. I asked him if he wanted to play catch with the football. Do you remember I told you I played football for the Forty-Niners for three weeks before breaking my arm? I see him eyeing the chainsaw while chewing a cereal bar slowly. I know he blames me for his mother's death, but it wasn't my fault the boat kept going. Your last e-mail was so helpful. It's great that you know other chefs like me because then you can really understand my problems.

Sincerely,
Richard McBeef

"You recognize that name, don't you?"

"Fuck."

"Why is someone with this name sending e-mails to you at work?"

"I don't know."

"Did you write this? As some fucked-up joke? I read some of your shit on the Internet. You have *Richard McBeef* and *Mr. Brownstone* down as two of your favorite books. That's some fucked-up shit, man."

"I have this friend Adam. He thinks these sorts of things are funny."

"Okay, man, I'm going to have to ask you to come down and answer some questions."

"All right."

4.   In Kim's car, I explained my guilt.

Richard McBeef was a one-act play written by Cho Seung-Hui, the twenty-three-year-old English major who would go on to murder thirty-two people at Virginia Tech. Just ten pages long and printed in a comically large font, *Richard McBeef* tells the story of a young boy named John, who, one morning over a cereal bar breakfast, confronts his abusive stepfather, Richard McBeef. There is no semblance of reason in the play, no buildup of tension, none of the narrative logic that allows us to reflect back on ourselves as linear, sensitive creatures. Instead, there are fits of spontaneous anger, wild claims of violation and molestation, a mother's schizophrenic confusion, a revelation that is not a revelation, and, in the end, the murder of a young child. It is, as Adam put it, the greatest, most horrific episode of *Jerry Springer*, ever. The mechanics are the same: We are told the problem in advance, we anticipate the buildup. When the man comes charging through the curtain, we understand that there is no time for explanations or nuance. Unlike *Springer*, though, where the spontaneity and the degradation of the violence usually make us laugh. There is no barrier between the reader and Richard McBeef. The violence is simply violence. There is no large bald security guard to whisk it away.

Kim drove silently and badly down Guerrero. He muttered something to himself before telling us about being in his mother's restaurant the morning of the shootings. It was five-thirty and his mother needed help unloading a vegetable delivery truck, so she called him and his little brother, who works downtown. The truck was late, so Kim and his little brother sat in the back office and turned on the TV, and there was a report on CNN about how a confirmed four students had been murdered at Virginia Tech, but that nobody knew anything at that moment. People have a misconception about detectives, Kim explained. They think because we deal with bodies and murderers on the daily that we are somehow desensitized to death. Really, the opposite is true. Nothing is more energized than a fresh corpse. When you're always around that energy, you can't help but get drunk off death. His mom kept yelling on the phone and his brother and he just sort of watched as the body count got higher and higher and then he saw that kid, the one with glasses, who had escaped say it was some Asian kid, and he already knew our people were fucked. The Chinese aren't creative enough, the Nips don't have the balls or the specific brand of Korean crazy, which is really just the same crazy as the Irish crazy, because both peoples come from small countries oppressed for hundreds of years by the assholes across the way. Both peoples grew up under the eye of the crown or the emperor and learned to suppress everything, especially anger, until they no longer could distinguish what was what, and could walk around angry without recognizing anger as anger. And the prescription for whatever else was drinking.

That's what we are, Kim said. We're the hybrid of Jews and the Irish. That fucking nutjob only confirmed what we all knew about our people, didn't he?

I didn't want to answer his question, at least not directly, and certainly not in front of Ellen, so I told him that I had gotten on a Long Beach–bound flight at JFK at 7:30 A.M. and for six captive hours watched the body count rise on the headset television. When I saw the kid who had escaped describe the shooter as "Asian," I looked up the aisle and saw the rows of glowing little TVs, all of them tuned to CNN. Of course, I knew he was going to be Korean. I've never talked to any Korean who didn't know.

Kim snorted and asked, You know other Koreans? I ignored him.

When the plane landed, I walked down the steps and onto the runway. I've always loved the Long Beach airport because you could shoot a film set in the fifties there and wouldn't have to change a detail. I remember, though, wishing that I had flown into LAX, so that I could sit entombed inside the guts of an airport for just a bit longer. Kathleen, my girlfriend at the time, was waiting for me and as we drove back up the 405 to her apartment in Westwood, she kept saying how awful it all was. Nobody was saying anything at the time about the shooter, except the few leaks that came out that said he was Asian. How could Kathleen have known what I knew, what you knew? And if I had tried to explain it to her, what could she have said? It all sounds so insane to me now. The next morning, when they posted his photo and his name, I refused to think about it. But I was glad, for the first time, that my parents were both dead.

When I got back to New York, I met my friend Hyung-Jae in a bar around Columbia. He asked if I had read *Richard McBeef* and *Mr. Brownstone*, and we talked about it without all the scorn with which we discussed all works of literature. I remember Hyung-Jae admitting that he had once thought about shooting one of his teachers, not in an abstract sense, but to the point where he went to Walmart to buy a gun.

We shouldn't be allowed, he said, to see ourselves like that.

On Wednesdays, the owner of that soggy bar would project the Yankees game up onto the back wall. We watched a few innings in silence. I think we both knew that we would never be this close again. A few days later, he forwarded me some post on a humor blog. It was a Lacanian critique of *Richard McBeef.* You will never convince me that someone other than Hyung-Jae wrote that. For the next few months, whenever I saw him, we would just make jokes about Virginia Tech and Cho Seung-Hui. The baseball season had just started up. We were both big fans. But we never talked about anything but Virginia Tech, and we never allowed ourselves to say anything about it that wasn't ironic or awful.

It was the worst day in our history, Kim said, and you fuckers made jokes about it.

What did you do?

I cried like a fucking baby. I talked my mother out of fleeing the country. I stood outside her restaurant at night for a week because she was afraid it was going to be Rodney King all over again. I gave money to the church around here even though I hate the Korean fucking church. You new kids, man. You grow up thinking you're white. But then when something happens that reminds you that you aren't, you got no way to respond. You just stand there stuttering and holding your cock as the white world evacuates all of its well-meaning bullshit.

Please, stop. I don't disagree with you.

Yeah, well, fuck you.

BOOK FIVE

218 A 39th Avenue was a flat-topped two-story stucco building whose color could best be described as moldy orange. A rusted-out Dodge Ram was parked diagonally across the driveway, blocking in two identical black Mercedes S-Class sedans. A modest scooter, the sort that looks natural only with twelve plastic bags of Chinese delivery saddled out to the sides, stood abandoned on the sidewalk.

Finch parked his car a few blocks away on Fulton. The dislodged, happy bird was still bumping around. He kept catching himself grinning. With one of these random grins on his face, he called the number the girl had provided.

She picked up before the phone had a chance to ring. "You're here?" She was whispering. In the background, Finch heard a TV.

"A few blocks away, as promised."

"Is your car easily accessible?"

"Sure."

"Okay. I'll be out in front of the house."

"Okay."

"Do you have your gun?"

"I can bring one, but you have to explain why."

"Can't now. Just bring one, please. It's not a big deal."

From the trunk of his car, stashed below the tub that held his wet suit, Finch pulled out his double-action 96D Beretta and its blond leather holster. He hadn't brought a jacket, so he unlatched the weapon and shoved it down the front of his pants. The sight of the butt of the gun sticking up out of the waist of his jeans struck him as incredibly funny, as if he had woken up from a deep slumber and found himself on the other side of the law. It occurred to him, vaguely, that he should call for backup, but in his state of spasmodic joy, he couldn't bring himself to pick up his radio.

He strutted up to the moldy orange house. With each step, the gun slid farther down his pants leg. He wondered how the black kids did it. Then, thinking of what Kim's explanation would be, he laughed out loud.

Lionface was standing on the stoop, huddled in a midnight blue kimono. She looked cold. Her hair, which Finch could have sworn had been brown and straight, was actually deep red, curly, and tied up in a bun atop her head.

Finch tried to summon up his memory of any part of her other than her two swinging breasts, but all he could muster up was a mole, although he couldn't possibly tell you which body part it had punctuated, and an abstracted face, which, had he been a bit more lucid, he would have recognized as that of the actress who played Juliet in the sixties film version of *Romeo and Juliet* they used to show in schools, despite the quick flash of nipples and an arty, anatomically impossible sex scene.

And had the circumstances not made it nearly impossible that the redhead waving on the stoop was, in fact, an incidental half-naked woman, Finch would have kept walking down the street. But when he nodded, she nodded back. He recognized the reassuring breadth of her cheekbones. She waved him inside.

Even from the sidewalk, Finch had picked up the heavy smell of skunk. By the time he walked into the house, the smell was so thick that he was forced to breathe through his mouth. Lionface was standing in the corner of a bare foyer, huddled forward with her hands gripped tightly on the sash of her kimono, as if anticipating some gusty, denuding wind.

Finch whispered, "I brought the gun. But you're going to have to tell me why."

Lionface put her finger to her lips and motioned her head at a flight of carpeted stairs.

Hand on gun, Finch followed her up to an unlit hallway. He counted three doors on either side, each one framed in a fluorescent glow. He could now feel the skunk down in his lungs. Lionface once again put a finger to her lips. Then, with those two hands trained in tenderness, she opened the first door on the right.

Finch's suspicions were confirmed. Inside, in what had presumably once been a bedroom, forty marijuana plants reached greedily up to their parent grow lights. Finch heard the opening bars to the Dead

Kennedys' "Holiday in Cambodia." In the back corner of the room he saw a couch wrapped in black plastic where two men sat, both propped up and unconscious.

The first was a thin, bearded man, who, at first glance, appeared to have vomited all over the front of his black hoodie. All he could see of the other man was a round bald head. The rest of his face was obscured by an airplane sleep mask and a gag, loosely tied.

Finch started to move toward the men, but Lionface stepped in front of him. Her eyes bulged. Finch arched his eyebrows and stuck his thumb out in the general direction of the street. She nodded and led him outside.

She kept walking once she hit fresh air, across the yard, down the block, across Fulton, and into Golden Gate Park. In a foggy clearing in the trees, she stopped, spun around, dug into one of the pockets of her kimono, and handed him a California driver's license.

She said, "Heather."

Finch looked at the driver's license: Heather Alejandra LeBlanc from San Clemente, CA. Born 10/2/1984.

"Okay, Heather, can you explain what that was back there?"

"Is it not obvious?"

"Why don't you tell me?"

"I thought . . . Well, I thought showing you would be enough."

The grinding condescension of the pop star acne medication hack had been replaced with a breathy, anachronistic tremolo. Finch didn't know what to make of this change, but it occurred to him that he should suspect something was up.

"Is anyone dead?"

"No."

"Who were those men?"

"You didn't recognize him?"

"Recognize who?"

"Mister Hofspaur."

"That was Hofspaur?"

"Bald head?"

"I'm going to have to go back there and look more closely."

"That's not possible."

"Why not?"

"Because they're going to come soon. I'm sure they've already noticed that the video cameras are down. Please, you have to help me."

"Who is they?"

"The same people who drugged you."

"Can you be more specific?"

"Well, for you . . . It was a mistake. They thought you were some other cop. But for the other guy, the pornographer"—she looked down, demurely, while pronouncing that word—"they've been planning this for a while. They want to scare him."

"They thought I was some other cop?"

"Bar Davis."

"Bar Davis is a woman."

"Well, they know that now. But they just assumed, you know, 'cause you were with the other guy."

"They thought I was Bar Davis."

"Yes. But they knew they fucked up when they checked your ID when you were passed out."

"And the other man back there?"

"The closest thing you could call him would be my boyfriend."

"What happened to him?"

"Once I knew you were coming, I drugged him."

"With what?"

"Lots of stuff."

"Well, I have to assess whether or not somebody is going to die."

There was a snap to their exchange that struck Finch as odd. It was as if they had already had this talk and were simply rehearsing it again, quickly, so each could head back home. For some reason unknown to him, maybe the residual effect of the drug, he licked his palm and slicked back his salty, stiff hair.

"So the other man is your boyfriend."

"You have to help me here. Please."

"Is there anyone else in the house?"

"I can't tell you right now. Please, can you take me down to the station or something?"

A distant look of reverie fell over Heather LeBlanc's face, as if she were trying to remember something from a happier past. Her eyes began to fill with tears. Her lip trembled. With a restored tremolo, she wailed, "I know why you're suspicious. You're right to be suspicious. Listen, I know why you don't trust me. I was back there in the café when they drugged you, and you can probably tell, just from your detective's eye, that I haven't lived a good life."

"What?"

"I've been bad."

"That doesn't matter, Heather. Why are you in danger?"

"I can't tell you. I can't tell you right now. You have to trust me. Be generous, Inspector. I know I have no right to ask you, but you need to help me."

"Well, I am a police officer, and therefore am bound by my—"

"Please!"

"We'll take you down to the station. You'll be safe there. We can sort things out. But first, I have to tend to those two guys in that house. You understand, right?"

Something buzzed. She nodded. They left the park. On the corner of 39th and Fulton, Finch's gun got dislodged from his waist and fell, barrel-first, down his left pants leg. Finch laughed again, but then wondered what might have happened to his brain.

When they got to the house, both of the Mercedeses, the old Dodge Ram truck, the boyfriend, and Hofspaur were all gone. Of course they were.

ANTE UP

1.   I answered all of Jim Kim's questions. It took about an hour. He didn't put me in an interrogation room or offer me coffee. Instead, I sat on a smelly couch in his office. His questions were mostly about work. I told him I didn't know anything more about Bill's clients than he did, but that the company must have Richard McBeef's credit card information on file. I told him no one who worked at getoverit.com had ever had any actual contact with a client. At least not that I knew of. We used fake names, made up fake friends, cut and pasted our advice from a database of reassuring words. I agreed that one of us probably did deserve to get killed.

As for Richard McBeef, I told Kim the truth: Despite the awfulness of making fun of it on a profile page, I never would have had the heart to summon up that name, especially to someone who wasn't specifically hurt by the menace of Cho Seung-Hui. Kim shook his head. His earlier disgust had been replaced by a grim, mechanized dickishness. The edges of his mouth never moved. His pencil kept tap-tap-tapping at the edge of his desk.

To answer Ellen's pleadings, Kim told us we probably weren't in danger. If I did not exist, the Baby Molester and Bill would be planets spinning in their own sad, little orbits. As proof, he pointed out that Bill had 573 friends across seven different social networks, and not one of them was friends with Dolores Stone. Bringing up one of my profiles, he pointed out that despite having spent his entire life in San Francisco, insulated by a tight-knit all-Korean social group, Kim's own little brother was friends with not one but two people who were friends with me. It was a weird way to prove our safety, but I guess it was reassuring to see even the slightest hint of math in our favor. "Unless *you* killed them both," Kim said, "there's no reason to worry. Besides," he reasoned, "if they wanted to kill you, they would've killed you outside the bar. These gangs, they don't kill witnesses like they do in movies. I mean, except when they do. But for the most part, taking civilian lives just gets us up their ass. They wouldn't just pop some dipshit because he was seen walking with some other dipshit who might have known something about some murder nobody is linking them to anyway."

"So," Ellen asked, "what you're saying is that this is a coincidence?"

"No," Kim said, "it's too early to say that. I agree, it's fucked up, but I don't think you two need to be running around fearing for your lives. Go home. Share a meal. I'll call you later tonight."

2. We returned to a gutted room. The tubs had been flipped, the bed stripped of its New England linen. All those lovely pastel bottles of hair and body products had been decapped and poured out into the shower. Even Ellen's gym bag had been violated, the aluminum water bottle drained, the shin guards sliced open. We found her field hockey stick under the bed. Ellen gripped it tightly as we searched in vain for anything that might be missing.

When every last lacrosse ball, every bit of lingerie had been counted, we sat on the edge of the bed, my hands shoved in the crevasse between her thighs. Ellen tried calling Kim, but went straight to voice mail. She left a detailed, polite message, explaining exactly what had happened. I cannot remember what went through my mind, at least not exactly. At some point, I started to rub the heel of my palm against the spot where my memory had mapped out her clitoris. In response, Ellen snorted. The room got dark. It was seven-thirty.

There was nothing left to do. Our panic and shock burned out. Both of us accepted our lot and wherever the lot might go.

We threw everything back into the tubs and went out to get drunk.

3 . Our first stop was at the breezy, yuppie wine bar up on 18th Street. Ellen took out her phone and placed it faceup on the bar. "I can't feel the vibrations anymore," she explained. "Especially when I get as drunk as I'm planning on getting." She ordered two bottles of wine and a cheese plate. I didn't have the heart to tell her that I was lactose-intolerant, but had just the shred of hope left to not risk a night of farting in front of my new girlfriend. She didn't notice, ate the whole cheese plate herself. Again, I was in love. We didn't talk about what was happening. Instead, she told me about her parents' vacation house in Mexico and the boys she met during her childhood summers. A bottle and a half in, she giggled and said that there had been times when she had wondered if her relationship with Mel was just her way of finding a white replacement for all those beautiful Mexican boys. Who has the heart to judge a girl who talks about sex while devouring cheese? Especially in my state? I just drank more and told her about the time I drove down with my friend Chad to a rope swing out in Pittsboro, North Carolina. It was a half-mile hike through poison ivy and all the greenish undergrowth that pops up in the South, the sort of generic, choking vegetation that never seems worth naming. As we walked up the river's bank, we could see little islands of pig shit floating on the surface of the brown water. Somehow, the cocooning greenness of the leaves, the redness of the clay, and the humidity in the air made even pig shit seem healthy. About a year later, while I was trying to show the first girl who had ever told me that she loved me the rope swing, a vacationing couple from Fort Lauderdale would rear-end my minivan and blow out the back windows. The girl gathered a handful of shattered glass and put it in an Empress typewriter ribbon tin because she had just watched *Breakfast at Tiffany's*.

Anyway, on that day I was just telling you about, Chad and I drove to the rope swing listening to Bill Withers's *Greatest Hits*. There was a thrift store on the way, and next to it, a soda fountain that served egg creams. We stopped in and looked for tuxedos for some school dance that was coming up. When we got to the turnoff for the rope swing, we parked and walked in, towels draped around our shoulders. But when we got to the spot, we saw a bunch of Mexican kids taking turns on the swing. Neither of us knew what to do. Were they black, we would've skulked back to the car. If they were white, we would've asked for a turn. Even then, I think both of us had been to too much school to realize that we had not, at the age of sixteen, ever dealt with a Mexican without the ease and padding of some service position, so neither of us could acknowledge the weirdness, and so we took refuge under a willow and silently watched them take turns climbing the boards nailed into the side of the tree—the sort of tree steps that could have appeared in *Pogo* or even *Br'er Rabbit*— as the Mexican kids, one by one, bombed themselves right, and I mean *right*, into the islands of pig shit. In the spring, every year, the white people would have a festival on that river, to save it from pig shit, and so when Kathleen finally asked me to the bluegrass festival where I first saw the Baby Molester, how could I have explained what, exactly, was churning in my heart? Just the jangly, kind crowd, the sight of old men and mandolins on the stage brought me back to the muddy spot where Chad and I stood on the bank of the river beneath the heavy droop of a hundred-year-old willow whose greenness is impossible to describe—if you cut Hermes open, his heart would be that green. After some hand-wringing, we decided to try again later and turned to walk back to the car. As we came out from under the willow, I saw one of the kids, his face glowing like a lucky moon, gesture us toward the tree. The other kids were all bobbing in the water, and they just grinned as I grimly climbed up the steps. The kid who had motioned us over handed me the rope, and before my cowardice could betray me, I jumped off. I don't know, it was like maybe fifteen, twenty feet off the ground, I didn't look down. My arms back then were just barely strong enough to support my weight, so instead of swinging out into the deep middle, I tumbled headfirst down into the shallow bank. You know those videos people send around of rednecks catching catfish with their arms? That's where I landed. No, I wasn't hurt, but when I came up to surface, those brown heads were bobbing nearby and each one was laughing at me.

My mother told me once to soften up my laugh. She could hear no forgiveness in it, no concession to the fact that we are all trying. I can think of the reasons why it ended up that way, but I've never been able to change.

That dickhead detective was right. When I laugh, it's because the world is suffering.

When I came up to the surface and saw the kids laughing, my mind locked into an ugly, eugenic calculus. Chad went hurtling over my head and splashed straight into one of those pig shit blooms. The laughter, once again, rang up the river. I remember pretending to be hurt, clutching at my knee to avoid looking back out at the river, or up at the branch, where the moon-faced kid still sat. Had I known what to look for, I would have seen the generosity my mother had always missed in her only son, the kindness you can only hope happens to your children, because while you can teach a person to act kindly, you can't really teach warmth.

From the willow tree, I watched Chad get along better with those Mexican kids. I couldn't come up with a comfortable, or even angry, reason why, so I just watched, excerpting myself so that the heat and the humidity and the greenness were no longer oppressive or sticky or even beautiful. Then, Smiley-Face Moon, who had since jumped down from the branch, ran over to a plastic cooler they had set on a stump. After rummaging around a bit, he pulled something out and trotted over toward my willow fortress. I stood up, vaguely scared, and screwed on a smile. He did a better job at it. You know when you meet someone who doesn't speak English and they give you this huge, silly grin, like they're saying, "Hey, I'm sorry we can't talk, but we're okay"? There's a lady who works in one of those doughnut shops–slash–Chinese buffets on Clement Street who smiles like that. It's always kind of breaking my heart—did I just use that phrase?—because she's always touching dirty things and not washing her hands. Anyway, this kid ducks under the willow branches, and guess what he hands me? A quesadilla in a Ziploc bag. I don't think I'll ever forget it. Me, standing there, humiliated, worried vaguely about how the unflattering fabric of my bathing suit was clinging to my shrinking, stereotyped penis, Chad making friends, and this kid brings me a fucking quesadilla in a plastic bag. I looked down at the tops of my bare feet and the little currents of pig shit river water dripping off my shorts, and, for that moment, I could press my hands up against the furthest edge of love. And it felt massive.

Even back then, I knew this sort of moment would have been better set in the fifties or sixties or even the 1890s, but in 1996 we all knew better than to say something silly and impolite, like, when I was seventeen, I met some Mexican kids on the banks of the Haw River and one of them handed me a quesadilla in a plastic bag. I'll never get the image of that quesadilla out of my mind, but I can't tell anyone that story and I certainly can't write about it because our modern tolerance assumes all cross-cultural exchanges are either zero-sum or simply amazing. You're supposed to write, at best, about foods, dances, weird clothes, and mothers who catch you with your cock in your guilty, yellow hands, but you're not supposed to write about the time when you became a bit less of a bigot. Because you already were supposed to have gotten through that.

We, you and me, were raised to assume our humanity.

She laughed. She said, "Maybe you were."

We got a bit drunker.

At some point, Ellen picked up her phone to see if Kim had called. A grizzled man smiled on the screen. He had on some sort of floppy sun hat. I would not have described him as looking happy, but I suppose, if fair is fair, I have never described anyone as looking happy. Ellen stared in at the man's face, not quite comprehending.

"That's mine. Your phone is over there." It was the bartender. Maybe it was all the wine and the soft light, but she looked, almost exactly, like Diane Lane.

Ellen placed the phone, screen up, in her open palm and offered it to her. She asked, "Is that your boyfriend?"

"Husband."

"Husband?"

"Yes."

"You're lucky. He's really hot."

The bartender plucked the phone out of Ellen's hand and stared in at the screen. She pursed her lips. Attractively. And sighed. Also attractively. Looking up at Ellen with those Diane Lane doe eyes, she said, "Thank you." And then, "I'm going to step away for a minute. You two good?"

Kim called Ellen's phone at around eleven. Her side of the conversation involved a lot of yeses and noes. After hanging up, she asked the bartender if she could turn the TV to the local news, and, perhaps, turn up the volume. Something important had just happened. The bartender asked if there had been an earthquake, but Ellen shook her head and just repeated the request. The bartender said she could turn on the news, but couldn't turn up the sound. Her manager, she explained. Ellen asked if she could at least turn on the captions.

<JULIE>: WEL-COME TO THE KCAL ABC ELEVEN O'CLOCK NEWS, I'M JULIE CHEN. SAN FRANCISCO POLICE TONIGHT RECEIVED A LET—LETTER FROM AN ORGANIZATION WHO CLAIMED RESPONSIBILITY FOR TWO MURDERS THAT HAVE TAKEN PLACE IN THE CITY OVER THE PAST WEEK.

THE VICTIMS, FIFTY-SEVEN-YEAR-OLD DOLORES STONE
AND TWENTY-FOUR-YEAR-OLD WILLIAM CURREN, WERE
BOTH FOUND DEAD IN THEIR APARTMENTS EARLIER
THIS WEEK. THE POLICE RELEASED A STATEMENT
TONIGHT REVEALING THE EXISTENCE OF THE LETTER,
AND, INDEED CONFIRMING THAT IT HAD BEEN SENT
BY AN ORGANIZATION CLAIMING RESPONSIBILITY FOR
THE MURDERS. HOWEVER, NO DETERMINATIONS HAVE
YET BEEN MADE AS TO WHETHER THIS CONSTITUTES
TERRORIST ACTIVITY. <PAUSE.> FOR MORE ON THE STORY,
LET'S GO OUT TO THE POLICE DEPARTMENT WHERE OUR
STREET REPORTER SAM ESTERMAN FILED A REPORT JUST
A FEW MOMENTS AGO.

<SAM>: THANKS JULIE. I'M HERE OUTSIDE THE POLICE
STATION DOWNTOWN. THERE HAVE BEEN REPORTS
COMING FROM SOURCES INSIDE THAT A LETTER
ARRIVED AROUND 2:30 TODAY FROM A GROUP CALLING
THEMSELVES THE BROWNSTONE KNIGHTS. AMONG OTHER
CRIMES, THE BROWNSTONE KNIGHTS HAVE CLAIMED
RESPONSIBILITY FOR THE MURDERS—

<JULIE>: SORRY WE'RE HAVING A BIT OF A MALFUNCTION.

The image on the screen had frozen. Street reporter Sam, bathed in
halogen, was standing on the steps of what I assumed was the downtown police station. His eyes had been frozen half closed, and his lip was
curled just enough to reveal a blurry but dazzlingly white set of teeth.

Behind his left shoulder, with, again, a blurry, malicious look on his dirty potato face, was Jim Kim.

I was too drunk to make much sense of it, but I do recall, for whatever reason, feeling relieved. I looked over at Ellen, but those fine, sturdy New England features weren't giving anything away. I considered telling her I loved her. The bartender, back from her break, said, "Holy shit. Jim Kim."

The bar's front door swung open.

It was Jim Kim.

The bartender said, "Jimmy. How weird. Look, you're up on the TV!"

He said, "Sarah. Where is your husband? I can't reach him on his phone."

Before she could answer, he looked me dead in the eyes and asked, "Did you recognize that name? Did you catch that name?"

I stared at the floor.

Mr. Brownstone. The name of Cho Seung-Hui's other play.

BOOK SIX

Heather stared at the vacated parking spaces, the open door, her face clouded in ruin. She whispered, "Whoever left here left in a hurry." Finch didn't ask who whoever was, but he had done the math. Two men, especially if one of the men lies unconscious and hog-tied, cannot drive away three cars, even if two of the cars are identical.

He asked, "Is there anyone else left in that house?"

She shook her head.

"Do you have any clothes in there?"

"I have some things."

"Well, why don't you get dressed and we'll go down to the station."

There was nowhere to sit in the Subaru, so Finch strapped his surfboards to the rack and tried his best to dust the sand off the passenger's seat. Heather's hair was now piled up like a conch atop her head, and she now wore a groovy yellow dress she had somehow found the time to accessorize: dull silver Mexican rings, a cloudy jade bracelet. To the unknowing observer, she could have been his young secretary.

He asked, "Where to?"

"Can we please go down to the station?"

"There are many stations."

"The downtown one."

As he pulled out onto Fulton, he asked her to explain everything she could explain. She said, "As I told you back in the restaurant, I was born in San Clemente, basically just in the last cluster of houses before you hit San Onofre. My father was a famous local shaper named Terry LeBlanc, and my brothers were—"

"I don't need your life story. Just an explanation of where we're going so that I can call in backup."

She looked hurt. Picking at some invisible thing on her bared knee, she said, "I was providing context."

They pulled up to the red light at Divisadero. He tried calling Kim, but went straight to voice mail. As he was about to call into dispatch, he heard Heather gasp. She was pointing at the intersection. The light had just turned green. The rusted-out Dodge Ram, flanked by the S-Class sedans, rolled into view. And then, much to Finch's dismay, one of the sedans went right, the other left. The Ram went straight.

Heather's gaping face gave nothing away.

Finch chose the Ram.

Through the Ram's rear windshield, Finch spotted a lone head bobbing up and down. Worried about being made, he instructed Heather to feel around the backseat for a magazine. When she came up with a copy of *Surfer's Journal,* he told her to hold it up in front of her face. There was still the problem of the beacon of her red hair, so he asked her to let it down. She heeded all these instructions without question or protest, and, as they followed the Ram down into the Western Addition, she appeared to be reading. On Fillmore, the Ram turned left. Finch, following three cars behind, called into dispatch and gave the girl the description of the three cars and the direction they were headed, but when Heather asked him what he was planning on having done, he realized he had no real idea.

On Geary, the Ram turned right and accelerated up the hill toward Gough. A white produce truck pulled out in front of the Subaru, blocking both the turnoff and Finch's line of sight. He cursed and felt around for his gun, which still was tucked into the waist of his pants. An old Asian man climbed down from the driver's seat and motioned for him to drive around. The traffic headed the other way was unrelenting, so Finch pulled onto the sidewalk, clipping one of his rearview mirrors up against a parking meter, and hurtled out onto Gough.

The Ram was gone.

FINCH LACKED THE confidence, and, perhaps, the aesthetic callousness, to start a high-speed chase in a Subaru Outback wagon, especially one with two surfboards strapped to the top, so he backed over the curb, parked, and got out. The passenger's side mirror dangled by its wires. It's like Van Gogh's ear, he thought to himself. Or something. Whatever. He was tired of thinking in metaphors and once again closed his eyes to feel around for the fish. But they were gone. He remembered a meal he had once had with his mother at some hole in the wall deep in the Chinese part of Daly City. His mother's acupuncturist and part-time lover had given the place his personal stamp of authenticity. When they got there, a curious Chinese woman with a perfectly round boil on her nose, a singularly immigrant blemish that conjured up the same mixture of disgust and wonderment he had found in *National Geographic*'s running gallery of tribal breasts, sat them down at a table by the window. Some malnourished-looking men were playing cards in the corner. The dank, suffocating smell of Nag Champa hung in the air. Upon being instructed by Finch's mother to "make it up as she goes along," the woman disappeared behind a curtain and returned with a Bunsen burner, a block of tofu, and a clay pot inside which a school of tiny fish darted around in a few inches of oily water. The woman lit the burner and placed the pot on it and watched, with a wicked smile, as the heat began to churn the water. Then, just as the water began to boil, she dropped the block of tofu into the pot. All the fish, sensing the coolness of the tofu, began burrowing their heads into the tofu. Within a few seconds, all the fish, save one, had entombed themselves in that white soy mausoleum. The woman must have seen the horror and the restraint on Finch's mother's face because she cackled, and then, with a magician's flourish, extracted the tofu and sliced it in half, revealing all the corpses inside. Had the catfish, with their spiny heads, chosen a similar grave? Had his brain become fish loaf?

THERE WAS NOTHING left to do. He called in the Ram and gave dispatch strict directions to call him the second any of the three cars were pulled over. He motioned Heather out of the car. They walked to a

nearby Panda Express. He ordered a bag of egg rolls and a soda and let
Heather finish her explanation.

"AS I WAS saying, I was born in San Clemente. You've seen *The Naked
Gun*, right? You know those boob buildings? Like five miles from those.
My brothers grew up on the beach, and by the time our father went away,
their sponsors had moved the oldest one to the North Shore, the middle
one to the Gold Coast. I was left alone with my mother. She never quite
got over what my dad used to be. I kind of understand, though. Even
during the worst of it, when the years of dust from the shaping room had
cut his lungs in half, when the meth had taken his teeth and his strength,
she'd always ask him if he was going to go surfing.

"What was I doing during that time? Oh, I don't know. I was eating
a lot of Metabolife and trying to think of a way to get out of there that
didn't involve doing better at school. I fell in love with one of my brother's
old friends, but he got pissed at me because he said I was looking at
another boy's pecs. That's what he said, 'You were looking at his pecs.'
When I laughed, he threw me in his car and wouldn't let me out until the
cops came. Then I dropped out of school and moved down to San Diego
with one of my girlfriends. One of my father's old shaping buddies had
offered us his extra room. He lived right on Mission Boulevard, in this
run-down duplex. From the bathroom window, you could kinda see the
ocean. We both stayed there a couple weeks. I got too drunk one night
and went for a walk down the boardwalk to the roller coaster at the end
of Mission Beach. There was a taco stand there, and I remember order-
ing five rolled tacos and a Diet Coke and sitting down on the seawall
with my back facing the waves. I knew if I stood straight up and walked

in a straight line through the marsh, I'd end up falling into Shamu's tank at Sea World.

"When I got back to the apartment, the front door was open and someone was crying inside. I saw my friend in the corner. My dad's old shaping buddy was laid out in the kitchen, bleeding from the head. I've never seen skin just hacked up like that.

"I didn't need to know anything. I went to the kitchen, took out a knife, and stabbed him right in the back. It's tough to stab someone with a kitchen knife. I'm sure you know that. By the time the police showed up, I had just made it through his shirt. The cops asked what had happened and we told them and when they looked up my dad's friend's record they saw he had been arrested three times for sexual assault and so we were let go after just a couple hours in jail. No charges were ever brought up, but we knew we couldn't be friends again.

"I moved up to San Francisco and started working as a hairdresser and then a dancer down on O'Farrell, and then there was one night when I was walking out of work after some fratty guy had puked on me during a lap dance. There was this quiet-looking man standing outside of a corner store who asked me where I was going and if I wanted to get a drink. He said his name was Karlos with a 'k,' and he spent the whole night talking about surfing and being abundance. Just the way he said the word was beautiful and hypnotic, the way the names of tropical places can convince you that nothing ever goes wrong there. What could go wrong in San Tropez? In Bali? Who doesn't want abundance? He told me he owned a restaurant and said he'd pay me to be a hostess there, but I'd have to stop stripping. This was three, three and a half years ago. I've worked there ever since.

"About a year and a half ago, this monk who said he had spent ten years on a mountaintop in Japan came and visited the restaurant. He insisted on washing dishes, but it was clear from the start that he had a hold on Karlos's mind. The monk kept talking about this concept he called Electronic Separation, where the constant interaction of mind with an energized source, in most people's cases a computer or television screen, was responsible for a worldwide evacuation of body energy. As evidence, he pointed out the city of San Francisco, which, he argued, was in ruins.

"It all made sense to Karlos. Of course it did. He began recruiting people who had been laid off in the tech industry. He'd log into tech job hunter websites, pretending to be a start-up called Brownstone Industries. When anyone replied with any pertinent information, he'd send one of us girls to go find these guys at bars or wherever, and we'd be asked to do whatever it took to get the talent on board. You'd be shocked how easy it was. It took five months, and Karlos had a crack team of programmers and hackers who were tasked with taking down a long list of soul criminals. Mister Hofspaur was near the top of that list.

"There's only a little left to go. The hackers started attacking employees of the companies. Karlos began devising plans to intimidate and terrify the executives. The list of targeted companies just kept getting bigger. We even started a campaign against a group of surfers who started some stupid website community to post surf reports, because Karlos thought they were monetizing and digitizing the ocean. The kidnapping of Mister Hofspaur was just the next step. It's going to get worse."

"This Karlos."

"Yes."

"Does Karlos have a last name?"

"His real name isn't Karlos. It's Robert."

"Robert."

"Yes."

"Can you describe Robert?"

"He's big. Brown hair. Broken nose."

"And he surfs?"

"Yes."

"Can you describe his board?"

"He has so many, but they're all red."

Finch heard a rumbling in his skull. Closing his eyes, he saw the catfish wriggling their way out of his brain. He let them all swim away. The joy that had been knocking around threw up its hands and dissipated. He heard his phone buzz, but he knew that what they had found no longer mattered.

He had his man.

"Where is he?"

"I don't know."

"Where are we going?"

"To somewhere with Internet."

THE REASON FINCH didn't call in for help, or even Kim, was that he had determined, with what he reasoned was 90 percent certainty, that Heather was lying to him. His suspicions had started when she had handed over her driver's license. It was a well-worn phrase down at the station, and not just in homicide, that if any witness gives you something, you might as well arrest the fucker. Maybe he didn't actually commit the crime, but at some point, that witness will turn on you.

Not only had Heather brought him to the scene of the crime, she had insisted on being taken down to the station. In all of Finch's years of work, no witness had ever volunteered to "go down to the station." It was a phrase born completely out of television's fantasy, and although many of Finch's dealings with witnesses were tinged with the influence of what they had watched on cop shows, TV's heavy hand had never quite pushed anyone to willingly entrap himself, or herself, within the stone walls of the downtown police station.

Then there was the issue of her life's story—why fill it in with so much humanizing detail? Why tell a cop so willingly about the time you stabbed an unconscious man in the back? Why say anything at all about your childhood? Sure, there was a surfboard strapped to the top of his car and he was wearing flip-flops, but Finch was not just a cop, but a cop she had drugged earlier that day. She had made herself a bit too relatable, a bit too easy to pity, and while he could attribute some of this to what must have been years of learning how to distill her angst through highly structured, intricately codified verbal diarrhea, he couldn't help but notice that her story was too structured, too shot through with loss, injury, and vague artiness, to be believable. The person she had described was what his wife, Sarah, would call a Noelle—a girl, best played by a melanin-deficient girl with bangs and big blue eyes, who whips up injury and a heavily affected quirkiness into a symphonic siren's song for all the lonely, doddering literary men to hear. My father did x and my response was not a response, but who can respond against all the y in the world, and so here I am with my beloved z, still addled by x, but trying my best to convince myself that $z > x + y$. Will you, my sad, literary w, will you add to my z, so I can be assured of the calculus of happiness?

The thing about Noelles, Sarah maintained, was that they were all fictions. Take a normal girl, deprive her of sunlight, dress her like a hobo, stretch out her eyes, cripple her in some way, teach her about the life of Kaspar Hauser, the catalog of Laura Nyro, and you have yourself a

Noelle. The only problem is that real life doesn't make golems out of all the silly, melancholy threads of our overeducated and oversaturated lives. Real girls, she said, want men to act like men. Anyone who pretends to like something different is just selling her soul to become another Noelle.

He looked over at Heather, her very red hair, and knew that she had no interest in becoming a Noelle. Rather, in Finch's detectivey opinion, it seemed as if she thought that he thought that she should be a Noelle.

That, Sarah would have argued, is the entire fucking point.

Where had she gone?

No matter. He pulled the Subaru in front of the Blue Danube Café on Clement. This time, he asked Heather to follow him inside.

IT WASN'T HARD to find Bad Vibes Bob.

BVB

Kelly Slater status

5832 posts

re: Save Sloat!

Broheims! Breaking rocks is tough work—I realize it would take away from your surf time but try and make the sacrifice. Back when I was kid at Malibu (1972), Don Redondo de Vaca came up from Sepulveda and stayed with us at Topanga for a week. He made us carry sand from the canyon to the beach—as it had turned out the waves that winter battered the coast and left nothing BUT exposed rock on the beach. The sand, I guess, had drifted towards Punta Conejo, Mexico . . . We thought he was nuts making us wear heavy army boots and heavy coats. And yes, we chanted and we chanted. I quit the name listing thing @ John Peck. Never got to Allen Sarlo. It was weird. Soon our parents got involved and they ran Don out of town. But you know what? We saved the beach! And that summer was the best porn surfing EVER! It is where I honed my front side style and attack.

Chant: BVB BVB BVB

BVB
Kelly Slater status
6315 posts

At the Point earlier this summer a couple a guys were on the outside chumping the shoulder so Billy and I watched and then COULD NOT TAKE IT ANYMORE! I had one guy out the back; cursing and trying to mount the fucker but he held me at a distance with his oar! There I am taunting him and he's being a fucking newly re-seeded hairline prick and I am desperately trying to pirate his SUP and he manages to stay on top of his board. I'm grabbing the rail, diving underneath a murky ocean and darned if I can't fucking dunk the guy. Meanwhile I'm missing all the good sets. He finally says, "You are being filmed . . ." I keep at him. Then he and his buddy (who in the meanwhile is busy with Billy) quickly paddle into the bay towards whatever drain and are gone. One hour later a policeman walks past our Peanut Gallery and then doubles back and stops in front of me and says, "Uh . . . were you surfing . . . a Paddle Boarder said that you told him that You were going to fucking eat his eye balls for dinner." To which I say, "I never said anything of the sort." Runs my license. Clean.

Each of the thousands of comments, littered across dozens of surf blogs, told the story of a pathologically insecure man who ground out his esteem in the unwritten rules of surf localism. And while the virulence and bad grammar of BVB's posts would make his mother weep with concern over her son's mental health and all those wasted tuition dollars, there was nothing explicitly criminal about his scrawled opus, nothing to indicate that this fight would be taken anywhere outside of the anonymous and guttering arena of a comments section.

But a codified confession wasn't what Finch was after.

He called the URLs into Goldwyn back at the station. About ten minutes later, he received the following text message:

172 PACIFIC. OLD NEIGHBORHOOD?

172 Pacific was just beyond the hill of Divisadero and Sacramento, where the mansions of San Francisco stand guard over the city with the same stony, timeless solemnity with which the menhirs of Stonehenge watch over the plains. Finch had grown up just three blocks down the hill, but still always held his breath whenever he drove through this boulevard of storied wealth. While his love of the underdog precluded him from thinking that the people who lived inside these houses were anything but monstrous (he had gone to school with almost all of their kids or grandkids, and they never shared their drugs or gave you rides in their mother's fancy car), he still appreciated the erratic circuitry of the city's old money, how there still seemed to be a spirit of eccentricity and silly patronage. Only in San Francisco did people still donate large parts of their estate to the opera. When the whole world is committed to saving the world, who will save the world?

THE HOUSE WAS just as nice as the other houses on the block—three of its five stories rose up above the roofs across the street, affording it a view of the hazy bay and Alcatraz and probably, if the owner of the house had invested correctly, the nameable beauty of the Golden Gate Bridge.

Heather, he noticed, wasn't even looking up at the address. She seemed to know where she was. In a new, throaty, Mae West voice, she said, "I have something to tell you."

"Okay."

"If you go into that house right now, you'll find Karlos and the monk and you'll have solved something that probably needs to be solved, but they'll think I helped you find them, and even if you agree to put me in witness protection, they'll find me because there's nowhere for me to go, really. So, if you choose to walk into that house, I won't be here when you get out and you'll never find me again, which means you'll have no one who can corroborate your version of things. I know the stuff Karlos says on the Internet is awful, but it's not a crime and so if you do want to pin them for beating people up and kidnapping Mister Hofspaur, you'll need me. Otherwise, all you saw was a pot farm owned by five people who have prescriptions who are just trying to grow a private stash, and a bald man tied up on a couch."

Finch didn't really know what to say to that. He pulled his phone out of his pocket.

It was a picture message from Sarah.

AS YET ANOTHER stipulation in their surrender to a pragmatic vision of love, Finch and Sarah had labeled text messaging as "strongly discouraged," especially during work hours. It had been Finch's idea. He couldn't stomach the anxiety of figuring out how to answer her texts (most were about grocery lists)—how to measure the appropriate response time, the humiliation of realizing that Sid Finch, city detective, handsome man, rider of waves, was almost always available to text back.

But here was not just a text message, but a picture message. His heart jumped.

Heather was saying something else about probable causes and fated outcomes, but Finch's attention was fixed on his phone's screen. The caption loaded first: WHILE YOU WERE GONE. And then, centimeter by blockish centimeter, an image unscrolled. The first bar was indecipherable—flesh tones against what appeared to be a green, almost oxidized backdrop. The second bar provided context—the curve of a waist, the pixelated suggestion of a belly button. A thin trail, grayish, tickled down from the belly button, almost as if an artist, exhausted after detailing the folds of the belly button, had simply let his pencil slip. Finch puzzled over the gray, wrote it off to bad cell phone camera technology, bad screen. The next two bars loaded in quick succession. The trail fanned out into a tangle of chestnut brown. The suggestion was enough—Finch, half seeing the matchbook-size picture, half seeing with memory, ran his eyes over the outer whorls, the paleness of the skin underneath, the furrows in the thick, curly hair near the lips. Those lips were dense, dark, permaswole—a bona fide furburger framed by two pony thighs. With the mild scent of her vagina filling his nostrils (he had always lamented this mildness because the smell never stayed for very long on his fingers), Finch recalled lying in bed with Sarah on their first night together. Once she had fallen asleep, Finch had turned on the lights, gently peeled back the top comforter, and stuck his head underneath the sheet. In that dank tent, the light filtering in through pale blue cotton, he had propped up his head with his elbow and stared for a real good minute at the whole thing. The vitality of Sarah's pussy—its fullness, its shocking wetness—convinced Finch of the health of all things Sarah.

That night, and for the next three years, there had only been a billy goat's beard, a comma punctuating the tip of her pelvis. The evidence, pixelated or not, of this new, unexplored thicket shamed Finch and confirmed the distance he had felt for years, really. Had Sarah's bush suddenly appeared in front of him, he would have reached both of his arms and embraced the fuck out of it.

FINCH SOUNDED A Bronx cheer and left her in the car. Fuck this. Who cared what Heather did? He walked up the steps and knocked on the front door of 172 Pacific.

CHRISTMAS APE GOES TO SUMMER CAMP

1.   One last thing about Cho Seung-Hui before I tell you what happened after Kim stormed into the bar. I wonder if anyone will ever really understand him in the way they tried to understand Dylan Klebold and Eric Harris. When the country saw two relatable kids walking through that cafeteria armed with Uzis, when they watched the videotapes of Dylan and Eric yelling about things their own kids probably yelled about, an explanation was demanded. With Cho Seung-Hui, his Koreanness/insanity was enough of an explanation, and so the talk eddied off. Nobody made an attempt to figure out what had possessed a twenty-three-year-old creative writing major, born in Korea, raised in the American suburbs, to suddenly open fire on his classmates.

I, at least, was never consulted.

What I am trying to say is this: If a kid like me makes monster tapes, sends them to NBC, and then walks into the engineering building to kill thirty-two people in the worst school massacre in American history and even he can't shoot his way out of the heavy blanket of cultural explanation, what hope do I, sad literary pussy that I am, have for an autonomous redemption?

So, when Kim stormed into the bar, yelling about Mr. Brownstone and some society of people who, I assumed, were part of the inspired generations for whom Cho Seung-Hui had died, I confess that my thoughts were not on Bill or the poor Baby Molester. My thoughts were on Cho Seung-Hui and how maybe someone was trying to understand him better.

For my sake, I hoped.

2. This is what Kim explained: Shortly after we left the station, he had received a call from a pay phone. The caller told him a letter would be arriving shortly via FedEx. Kim was to follow its instructions carefully. Sure enough, at that moment, one of the mail guys walked by and handed Kim a FedEx letter package. Inside, there was a blank envelope, and inside the envelope was a torn-out sheet of yellow legal paper with the following handwritten note.

We the Brownstone Knights claim responsibility for the murders of Dolores Stone and William Curren. We will bury anyone else who facilitates the degradation of our world. These two targets were chosen very specifically to send a message. Take heed, all others associated with the systematic degradation will also be taken out.

*Tell the world about us on the local news or
someone else will die.*

*Signed,
The Brownstone Knights*

He had done all the cursory checks, but could find no evidence of an organization calling itself the Brownstone Knights. The call was traced back to the Montgomery BART station, which meant nothing. As for our ruined hotel room, Kim said he couldn't even begin to speculate why the Brownstone Knights would harass me.

But he said he would drive us to the Fairmont Hotel and assign a patrol.

3.   At the Fairmont, we ordered scallops, champagne, and porn because Ellen said the only thing more sinful than waste was wasting luxury. For our patrol—a square-shouldered lesbian with a harelip—we ordered a Kobe burger and a sensible bottle of sparkling water, but she wouldn't even look at us, choosing instead to stare straight ahead at a corniced lamp that sat on a table by the elevator doors. We left her in the hallway and quickly forgot she was there. Ellen ate the burger, again citing waste, but I had noticed a bit of a teeter in her and desperately needed to know if it was just the stress that accompanies fearing for your life, or if she was actually in love with me.

When *SportsCenter* began to repeat itself, we flipped over to CNN.

It was three in the morning. I made a halfhearted attempt to kind of fall into Ellen's arms and brush my lips up against hers, but she said she had eaten too much for all that. There were rainstorms in Los Angeles. A small plane carrying a nature photographer and his three sons had gone down in Colorado. No confirmed word of any survivors. After the break we were going to see some shocking footage of a scene from downtown San Francisco.

I looked over at Ellen. She was gnawing on the corner of her napkin. A kitty litter commercial came on, a cat holding its nose with its paw. Napkin still hanging from her teeth, she turned to me and smiled.

The anchor returned and reminded us that before the break, she had promised us footage from a truly bizarre and "only in San Francisco" scene that had happened earlier today. James Sanders, a forty-six-year-old native of San Francisco, had put on an impromptu fashion show that was caught by several cell phone cameras. In a shaky frame in muted cell phone camera colors, which, if we dare to be so unsentimental, are the same colors as Monet's colors, was James. He was strutting down Market Street in a full-length fur coat and a pair of teal stilettos. Marching next to him, grimly holding his sign, his eyes blocked out by a pair of oversized sunglasses, was Frank Chu. I heard Ellen gasp. The next shot showed the duo farther down Market toward the gay Safeway, at the spot where the Burger King marks the border between the mall district and the crack district. James had changed into skintight leather pants and a T-shirt that had the words I'M TOO SEXY written in rhinestones across his chest. Frank Chu, still grim-faced and protesting, now wore a cabbie hat and a pair of white dinner gloves that disappeared into the cuffs of a voluminous, dazzlingly white tuxedo shirt. The banner at the bottom of the screen read:

VIRAL HOBO MARKETING? HOMELESS MAN PUTS
ON FASHION SHOW IN DOWNTOWN SAN FRANCISCO.

In the last video, shot from behind, James and Frank Chu, both dressed in somewhat tasteful bondage leather, disappear over the crest of the hill on Octavia. The Safeway sign hovers on the horizon, but you can still read the words printed on the back of Frank Chu's sign, the side he has always rented out to advertisers:

BEING ABUNDANCE CAFETERIA

I heard Ellen shift around in the bed. A pillow thudded against the TV. In a voice quivering with joy, she said, "That motherfucker was wearing my shoes."

4.   At four in the morning, seated amid a litter of room service plates, wine bottles, and coffee platters, we finally came up with our plausible scenario. James had tossed our room at the Hotel St. Francis because he needed a pair of women's shoes for his fashion show. The reason he did this, we deduced, was that he was insane. The attack outside the Uptown had been the spillover from the Baby Molester's murder. Because the party responsible was a terrorist group, which, we assumed, was primarily concerned with promoting its agenda, there was no reason why they would take the time and energy to track me down again. Someone probably had to pay, sure, but we couldn't find any reason it had to be us. As for Bill, we chalked it up to coincidence, and I marveled again, with my new girl, at the smallness of San Francisco and said some nice, smart things about how this Internet media social networking fuckanalia had done some crap and made some things that seemed impossible more possible, simulacra, planets spinning in their own orbits, and so on. We poured out a drink for the Baby Molester and Bill and said some nasty things about the vermin who would kill a destitute old lady and a decent dude, after which we screwed quickly and quietly, so as to not disturb our bull dyke patrol. Then, blessedly, entombed in Egyptian cotton, scallop juice, finer plates, and wine, we fell asleep.

We were wrong, of course, but a most-plausible scenario is still a most-plausible scenario, and when you're in love and fearing for your life, you accept any scaffolding upon which you can hang your fragile, contingent future.

5. Writers are always complaining about how Tolstoy ruined love. What they mean isn't that he gutted our expectations for romance, or cast an unrelenting eye on our vanities. It's more that after reading *Anna Karenina*, you realize the futility and clumsiness of any attempt you might make at projecting love, or even the concept of love, onto the printed page. He's just too good at it, and anything you try is doomed to sound silly, glib, or, even worse, *baroque*. In fact, the space Tolstoy takes up in the literature of love is so monstrous that if one were to draft up a list of the five best-written love stories, it would read something like this:

1. Vronsky and Anna (*Anna Karenina*)
2. Levin and Kitty (*Anna Karenina*)

3. Romeo and Juliet (*Romeo and Juliet*)
4. Isaac and Rebecca (Genesis)
5. Swann and Odette (*Swann's Way*)

I'm sure there are those who will protest the fact that three of the four authors are dead white men (I won't get into jokes or debates over the fourth), but dead white men invented romantic love, and so it seems reasonable that they would be best equipped to write about it. If someone were to draft a list of the greatest relationships between a man and, say, the reflection of the moon in a cup of wine, or anything involving mountains or farewells, the top fifty would all be Chinese. This doesn't mean that we can't find value in Thoreau, or even Pound, with his ornate imitations, but if you're looking for a pure distillation of something, especially something poetic, I say go straight to the source.

I'm stalling and deflecting, sure, but I am also trying, despite this weighty, ornate hesitation, to commit, at least to the written page, exactly what happened when I woke up in the morning and saw Ellen sleeping next to me—her arm flung dramatically across her forehead, her fingertips dipped in a puddle of mustard. I, who had always prided myself on my ability to accept the fallacy of love, with all my commas, parentheses, and qualified statements, felt love grab me violently by the back of the neck and fling me straight into her arms. This blooming helplessness, which flooded me to my teeth, made me feel a lot of different things, but mostly, it made me feel like a girl.

She was the eighteenth or nineteenth girl who had shared a bed with me. At least, in some way that counts. Early riser, always, I have watched each of these girls sleeping, and although I could usually muster up a flare of sentiment over the beauty of vulnerability, or whatever, I could also feel the slight but utterly evident discomfort of a forced appreciation, something similar to the tyranny that made me put Romeo and Juliet up on that list, when my real choice at number three would have been the off-page romance between Holden Caulfield and Old Jane.

But with Ellen, I only felt the need to gently lift those fingers out of the mustard puddle and wipe them off with a napkin dipped in water. She screwed one eye open. With a giant shit-eating grin on my face, I held up the yellowed napkin and chuckled.

How else could I explain love? I am compromised, in so many ways.

6 . Kim came by the room shortly after Ellen woke up. The hard edge from the Starbucks had been dulled down to something close to mere rudeness. More than anything, he seemed worried. I wondered if this show of vulnerability was some cop trick, or if, as I suspected, it was the sort of sign one immigrant flashes to another when he admits that the country cannot be conquered alone. Before his debriefing, which consisted of no new information and could have been easily done over the phone, he handed me a folder of e-mails printed from Bill's account. There were about fifteen in all, each one authored by someone calling himself Richard McBeef or Mr. Brownstone. He wanted me to see if I could detect some unfamiliarity with the language, some syntax that might provide us with a clue about the author.

As Kim fiddled with his keys and explained something to Ellen, I read over the letters, but they were all senseless, synthetic. Whatever awkwardness Kim had read in the sentences probably came from the pressure of having to cram so much of *Mr. Brownstone* and *Richard McBeef* into such a small epistolary space.

It was nice to feel useful, to say the least.

We explained our plausible scenario. Using Ellen's phone, we showed him the videos of James strutting down Market Street. Kim shook his head, glowering at the floor, but said we might as well stay at the hotel for a couple more days. The danger, he agreed, had passed. He would get in touch with us once he figured anything out and urged me to keep thinking about the letters, Cho Seung-Hui, the Baby Molester, and any possible connections between them all. If I came up with anything or remembered anything, I should give him a call.

Then, hangdogged, he left.

As Kim left, our guard cop entered the room and introduced herself as Officer Bar Davis. She apologized for being brusque the night before—Kim had explained the new scenario, and now that the threat seemed less imminent, she could ease up a bit. She said to ask if we needed anything.

We ordered breakfast up to the room: Eggs Benedict, something called morning steak, pancakes, and mimosas. Staring at the bubbles in the champagne flute, it dawned on me that I had been drunk for two or three straight days now. The thought made me giggle. Ellen, sawing through morning steak, looked up and smiled. She said, "The bubbles tickle my throat, too."

After breakfast, we had lazy, careless sex and watched *The View*. I checked my e-mail on my phone, but it was just the same silliness from Adam about who had published what where and how we were both fucked for life. The noon news started up. The anchor said something about a rash of murders with a possible link to an activist group within the city, but my plausible scenario was working its magic and I had no concern anymore. But then someone said something about funeral arrangements, and I looked up and saw a blue screen with these words.

FUNERAL OF DOLORES STONE
FOREVER HOME CEMETERY
TODAY AT 2:30 PM
COLMA, CA

Please send all donations, remembrances and thoughts to

MILES HOFSPAUR
433 Mission Street
San Franicsco, CA 94103

It seemed like a good way to put a close on all of this. Ellen must have been thinking something similar because she raised her questioning eyebrow.

But what to wear?

7.   Officer Davis dropped us off at Fight Against the Dying of the Light, a vintage shop on 16th and Mission, just up the street from the Hotel St. Francis. I've always loved shopping with girls, probably because the girls who end up with me are never the type to drag their men anywhere, especially somewhere with forgiving lighting and clean floors. Sitting on some couch, waiting for a girl to emerge from behind a curtain, is the edifying sort of torture that helps us understand generic stand-up comedy and the norms of American domesticity. For someone like me, who has lived so far outside of the narrative of paying taxes or the annoying guy who sits by the water cooler at work, these pauses of normalcy are my glimpse at what it might be like to be a bro. And so, slouching in a velvet love seat, I tried to look disinterested, and, more important, oppressed, every time Ellen came flouncing out from behind the curtain, but in my heart, I was happier than I've been in years.

Under the watchful eye of Doreen, the terminally thin, limping owner, Ellen tried on five different black dresses. Doreen kept fussing over the breadth of Ellen's shoulders, noting that in her day, girls didn't have four separate muscles in their arms, but after a good half hour, the three of us settled on an airy, lacy thing, a pair of black satin gloves, and a squared-off, almost Quakerish hat. For me, Doreen picked out a heavy wool suit with wide lapels, which she matched with a broad yellow power tie.

I won't mention how much it all cost, because that would ruin it, but as we were paying, Doreen told Ellen that a bright shade of lipstick was the key to looking good at a wedding, and, before the New England in Ellen could register a protest, Doreen grabbed her by the cheeks and smeared on a shade of red that would have made even Dolores Haze blush.

8 .   The burial plot was atop a steeply banked hill. From the car, we could only see the outlines of three men, each one standing with his hands clasped behind his back. Before starting the vertical ascent, I looked over at Ellen and saw she was frowning, though not sadly. If I were to guess at it, I'd say that she was probably hating California and its modern, spacious cemeteries and the good weather that always accompanies a funeral. At least, that's what I was thinking.

Anyway. I grabbed Ellen's hand, and we trundled up the hill.

Up top, we saw a party on the verge of breakout. The three respectful men were, in fact, security guards. On the far edge of the plot, four scraggly dudes were fiddling around with a PA. A guitar and a drum set lay in the grass behind them. A stand-up bass had been propped up against a gravestone. Surrounding a folding table stocked with handles of Costco booze were six or seven men with fuck-you-Dad piercings—septa, cheeks, foreheads—and tribal facial tattoos. I counted seven, maybe fifteen dogs running around, yapping at one another, and at least twenty or so old hippies, each one dressed in his or her referential, *Harold and Maude* best, smiling and drinking out of red plastic cups. Around the hole and the chains and the crane, a circle of women took turns staple gunning daisies to the coffin. All the young women had been surgically enhanced. Just beyond the coffin stood a line of grim-faced Latino kids, each one of them around high school age. Other than me and Ellen and the security guards, they were the only people dressed in anything resembling funeral attire, and, like us, they seemed to not really have any idea of how to react to this particular morass.

We hid behind the security guards. I couldn't tell if Ellen's hand was trembling in mine, or if mine was trembling in hers. But then she whispered, "Oh, my God," and I followed her eyes and saw, at the end of the line of Latino youth, the glowering face of the Advanced Creative Writer.

9.   Our plausible scenario was fucked, but I couldn't quite parse out whether it was fucked in a bad way. Before I could decide, a chubby bald man walked up to us with an offering of two red Dixie cups. I accepted mine and drank down half of whatever was inside. He smiled and said, "It's just vodka and cranberry juice. Don't worry."

Ellen smiled, tightly, and took the cup from the bald man's hand.

"So," he said, "how do you know ol' Dolores here?"

One of us said, "We were her neighbors."

"Ah, you can't beat a real neighbor. Especially these days."

"Yes. I guess that's true."

"How long have you two been living together?"

She winced. I tried not to think about why.

I said, "Not that long."

"Well, good luck to you. I apologize for the freak show. I'm sure you knew Dolores wasn't your average old lady, and her friends, as you can see, certainly don't fit that bill."

"It's not a problem."

"Well, I would hope not." Turning to Ellen, he asked, "So, what's your getup here? Jackie O at the funeral? Little Asian John-John?"

"Uh, yes. I am from Boston. The Boston area."

"You rarely see it go this way, Asian boy and corn-fed girl. It's always the other way around. Makes no sense to me. I say let the high achiever be the breadwinner. Why let all that work ethic go to waste?"

Despite myself, I laughed. The bald man smiled warmly and said, "This one knows what I'm talking about. I suppose it's the media's fault, especially media like me. I don't think we've filmed one single Asian male interracial scene, except when we gave Hisanori a little gift for his fifth-year anniversary with the company."

"Who?"

"Shoptalk. I'm boring you, but what beautiful half-Asian children you two will have. I'm not just saying that, by the way, because I've seen some monstrous and even some fat half-Asians, but I'm saying it because he has the face of a scholar and you, madam, are clearly descended from noble stock. There's just no way to miss. Mazel tov!"

"Thank you."

"All right, then, once I catch your names, I'll introduce you to everyone."

"My name is Ellen. This is Phil."

"Miles Hofspaur. And now, let's go introduce you to some people."

10.   Miles Hofspaur introduced us to Jennifer Rabbit, Blonde Ambition, Crystal Brandy, Preston Page, Prince Albert and the Knights of Ram-a-Lot, Lily Love, Larry Love, Alex Burns, and Anita Richard, who would be replacing Dolores as lead singer for the electric funk band Consciousness. We met all the old hippies who had names that could not have been real and the security guards before Miles brought us over to the Latino youth and took us down the line, introducing us to David, Oscar, Ignacio, John, Simon, and, finally, David, the Advanced Creative Writer.

"These fine young men," Miles said, gesturing down the line of sweaty kids in ill-fitted suits, "are Dolores's passion, her *corazón*. What a saint she was, no, boys?"

David, Oscar, Ignacio, John, Simon, and David, the Advanced Creative Writer, nodded. I felt kind of bad for them, shifting around nervously, trying not to react in any way to the surrounding insanity. There's nothing as stifling and infuriating as a well-intentioned, garrulous white man who is trying very hard to introduce you, his unexpected minority associates, in his best, most graceful way. Despite not knowing what to make of David the Advanced Creative Writer's blank stare, I felt the urge, paternal, I guess, to corral them around me and scream something about how they didn't need to feel like this white man was doing them some favor by showing off his magnanimous airs.

"Dolores," he continued, "our saint, gave her life to the city orphanages. These are some of her children, all of them fine young men who have come out to respect someone who was so important in their lives."

He led us away, back toward the folding table with the booze, and then left to go greet another couple. I poured out a quarter handle of gin into our cups. We sipped quietly amid the cheery talk, the bang of the staple gun, and the jangle of the band warming up. Ellen said it first: "Well, I guess the liberals are right."

"Yeah."

"He thought we were just ogling the murder scene."

"In his defense, we were."

"So where does that put us?"

"Let's figure it out later. Try to enjoy this."

"Okay, and will you look at that girl's ass? Are you even into that sort of thing?"

THE BAND PLAYED its first discernible chord, and everyone hushed and turned their attention to Anita Richard, who was standing in front of the microphone. She had changed into full bondage gear, and as the band rattled through the opening bars of "Play with Fire," she kept time, badly, by snapping her bullwhip. But she had a believable snarl and stalked around the grass, and it was the sort of trying too hard that stops short of being pitiful. I, at least, could appreciate the spectacle. And the drummer wasn't bad. At all, really.

After the requisite five-minute jam session at the end of "Play with Fire," which involved Anita Richard crawling on all fours and licking the air, a stumpy old lady walked up to the microphone and cleared her throat. She was wearing an ankle-length prairie dress, complete with quilted pockets and overly laced hem. A tuft of gray hair hovered over her tiny skull, not as if it were part of her, but more as if it were something entirely different that happened to be following her around. She introduced herself as Dolores's sister and pulled out a stack of note cards from one of those quilted pockets. A light applause scattered through the crowd.

Clearing her throat again, this time a bit indecently, she said, "Thank you all for coming here today. I am meeting almost all of you for the first time, but there is real love here and I find comfort in the fact that my sister lived amidst such beautiful and vibrant people.

"When we were girls growing up in Bakersfield, Dolores would always ask what I was going to say at her funeral. The question never carried the tone you might expect out of sisters—wistful, loving, with implied white-haired women who only say wise things, men lost to noble causes or noble illnesses, thick blood, beautiful hats, and varied grandchildren. There was none of that. Instead, I felt the hardness of a demand, a tinge of moral superiority, as if she was asking when I was going to hurry up and return her one good tartan dress, the one I couldn't quite fill out. What could I have said? She was the brown, leggy, forever California girl who could have doubled as both Ms. Seaside Pier and Ms. Brushfire Awareness. I was the older, mawkish brunette whose stockings rumpled, whose forehead protruded that disastrous half inch too much, the girl who floats face-first in the pool at the end of Act One.

"When we met up a year ago for a cousin's funeral, she asked if the eulogy had offered up any inspiration. She didn't explicitly say it, but I knew what she was implying. I reminded her, a bit too wryly, that the eulogy had been based on the life cycle of the salmon, and that for someone who had done what she had done, there was no returning to the home stream. She took it badly—she always took my deflections badly—but it wasn't anything that hadn't happened over the previous sixty years.

"Now that the time has come for me to say something, I predictably find myself at a loss. Not because I have nothing to say, but rather because there's nothing I can tell you, her life, her assembled mob, that you don't know better than I do."

She stopped there, and, for the first time since starting speaking, she looked up from her notes. Her eyes were calm, the color of beach stones in winter. We all heard the wind rattle through the snare drum, and somewhere, off on another hill, a lawn mower started up. The Baby Molester's sister seemed crushed by this intrusion. But when the moment passed, she continued.

"Dolores lived more, yes, but it was my idea for us to move to San Francisco. This was 1967, two years before the Summer of Love. I had just graduated from high school. Dolores was sixteen. The angst of all those pale, sharp-elbowed years had spun out into a grim, tightfisted dream of becoming a poet. San Francisco, as I understood, or, I suppose, misunderstood, was where a girl should go to become a poet. Dolores at sixteen was just like Dolores now and Dolores at twenty-six, but in Bakersfield, 1967, there weren't too many ways for vitality to be contextualized. She slept around. She sometimes walked in front of our stepfather in her underwear. But there was nothing unusual about this, except that she did all these things without the slightest hint of theater or remorse. Most beautiful women are crippled in some way by their power. Dolores just used it, never to get ahead, but just to use it because it was there.

"Maybe that's why she got San Francisco when I never could. Why the vacant spectacle of the Panhandle never bothered her. For those first few years, we did the same unbelievable things. We took acid and sat on the Dead's stoop in the Haight. We raised our fists with the Panthers. We came under the influence of terrible men. We drove to the desert and talked about death, Native Americans. From all that, I cordoned off a harsh little plot of judgment. My poems grew out of that acrid soil. Truth be told, I would have done the same thing had I stayed in Bakersfield. Instead of poems, I would have just raised miserable children.

"Dolores never cared much for my strangled, constructed things—I remember taking her once to City Lights to watch John Ashbery read "Farm Implements and Rutabagas in a Landscape" and "Donald Duck in Hollywood." She shifted nervously through all of it, but after I had introduced myself to Ashbery and curtsied—curtsied!—Dolores and I got cappuccinos and cannolis at an Italian bakery up across the street from the Roaring 20s. I remember she took her cannoli and just stood it up in her coffee cup and left it steeping as I tried to explain to her all the postmodern wonders of Ashbery's poems. When I was done, the cannoli sogged down, Dolores said that it must be nice to be in love with a man who had such an organized brain because it provides comfort for the future. That was my sister, always cutting right through it all to lay me bare.

"Of course, I was in love with Ashbery, and that was the point—think of poor ol' Borges, who arranged the world so symmetrically and geometrically, creating these perfect little prose engines and then gifting them all to his old loves. But I hated her for bringing emotion into it, to dismiss the height of my intellectual vanity for what it was.

"I'm not so naive to say that the ideas Dolores believed in were real, even back when they were conceived, but they at least were ideas. Those ideas have devolved into rationalizations—peace, love, and happiness is why the kids get excited about the new Eritrean restaurant, why they take photos in Thailand. Free love is vibrator slogan. Equality has become a way for certain rich people who have money and a certain education to pit themselves against other rich people. This is not news to anyone.

"And yet. Seeing you all here today, each one of you trying so hard, I can still feel the cold hand of reason on my neck: how cliché, these efforts, how useless, these desires. Here we are, even me, this cloistered false hippie, celebrating this depraved woman's life. And although context, history, forces me to acknowledge that people are people are people and my sister was my sister was my sister, in Bakersfield or on the moon, I can't help but wonder what all of you might have looked like had we never moved to San Francisco to participate in whatever it was that happened. My place at this funeral was fated long ago. You were the variable."

She cleared her throat once more, but whatever it had been that had inspired her words wouldn't rev up again. She sat, quietly, back down.

Ellen, I noticed, was crying. Sobbing, really.

I asked, "What's wrong?"

She said, "This just reminds me of something. From high school. Don't worry—it's not anything you have to understand."

The band, perhaps sensing a moment, stumbled through the opening bars of "Leaving on a Jet Plane," and the old hippies sang along, teary-eyed, and I wondered if anything had ever been so aesthetically objectionable and culturally inert as a bunch of old hippies singing a Peter, Paul and Mary song at the funeral of one of their old freaky San Francisco friends. And still, I thought about my mother, who would have been around their age, and her stories of protesting the Vietnam War in the streets of Seoul, and despite my attempts to suppress negativity, for Ellen's sake, I recalled the words of that fat, bald, gay music professor on how my father lacked the cultural heritage to understand *Blonde on Blonde*.

Whenever I summon up that memory, I picture my mother wandering around the basement of the music building at Bowdoin, maybe at graduation, maybe during one of those disastrous parents' weekends, lost in the linoleum, the industrial shelving, the blond oak doors that led into the small practice cubicles, and everywhere the smell of Ajax and spit valve. She had a habit of staying lost when she got lost as if wandering aimlessly was a condition that required no maintenance. During a trip to Mount Washington, she simply disappeared on a trail, and after six hours of searching and frantic chopped-English descriptions given to passersby and park rangers, we found her sitting cross-legged on the hood of our station wagon. A pile of dandelion roots lay in her lap. She didn't seem to comprehend our hysteria because all she said was, "I dug these up with my keys. We can make tea out of this, believe it or not." There were other times like this, and by the time I turned twelve, we simply let her wander off, knowing we'd always find her back by the car. And so, although she died four years before I left for college, it's logical or, perhaps, empirically validated to picture her wandering around the basement of the music building, the only place on campus where she might bump into Professor MacArthur, who, despite his grandiose bullying, was rarely seen anywhere else. He asks if she needs help finding something and she pauses to think it over and he will wonder if this tiny woman understands the question and so he asks again, louder and slower. She will smile and ask who he is and he will tell her and she will ask if he's ever taught her son, Philip Kim, and he will thrust out his hips, in recognition, and say, yes, yes, he's a bright boy and we talk about music quite frequently. She will ask if he's the music professor who is always going on about Bob Dylan. His hands will dig into his pockets, his hips will again rock forward, and his mouth will twist into his best, magnanimous smile. Here is a nice man, she will think, about my age. She will say something clumsy about "Blowing in the Wind," and he will be careful and smile and nod and think the best liberal thoughts about sharing and the cultural exchange and maybe he will ambitiously invite her up to the music library, his other sanctuary, where he can be found every afternoon with his oversized hi-fi headphones, listening to some jazz record from the private collection he so graciously has lent out for supervised student consumption. Maybe he will sit her down at a listening carrel, snap the headphones over the black satin headband she always wore on formal occasions, the touch of a woman who was always concerned with *subtlety*, and play her "Visions of Johanna" or "Ballad of Hollis Brown," just to watch her face crumble with the embarrassment of something loved that was then found to be something else, a bigamist of a memory.

I've pictured myself killing him again and again, and sometimes it convinces me that I am sick, but mostly it convinces me that I am a citizen. I hope you can understand why.

MY HAND STILL cradling Ellen's hand, I tried to hold off another on-coming memory, but it rammed up against my ribs, insistent as a shark's nose. Breathing in through my nostrils, I tried to feel drunker, and then, less drunk. Writers, for years, have been trying to figure out how to properly depict the fleeting, truncated, and always segmented nature of memory, but what about when it just up and crushes you straight in the sternum?

Those mornings in the parking lot with my three friends, the Ronizm mornings: Seth Bloomberg picked me up at seven-twenty on the dot. Our precalculus class started at eight-ten, and the teacher, an obese fading blonde named Ms. Butler, who, as if to hold up a stop sign against our pity, was always telling stories about her accountant husband, strictly forbade tardiness. At the time, Seth and I carried around the proofs of our delinquency as our best offering to the outside world, but we both still agreed that it was probably important, or at least elite-bohemian, to get into a good college. It was only a fifteen-minute drive from my house to school, but there was the five minutes it took to roll a joint, the five minutes to slowly roll through the main avenue of my subdivision while smoking the joint, the eight to ten minutes it took for us to get break-fast sandwiches at the Wilco, and the ten or so minutes we spent in the school's parking lot with our other two friends. Seth drove a safety-orange 1974 Volvo inherited from his dead grandmother, who had just used the car to shuttle back and forth from the one kosher grocery store over in Durham. The speakers were fragile and snapped irritably every time we tried to play anything with more than a teaspoon of bass. This was a problem. All we listened to back then was gangster rap. Looking back, I wonder if I might have missed out on part of the point of "Straight outta Compton," *The Chronic,* or *Doggystyle,* because until I left high school, I had never heard those songs and albums, or any of the West Coast trunk bangers, with even a percentage of the required level of bass. Does "Fuck tha Police" ring less true if Cube's voice gets all tinny because the only way you can turn up the volume is to crank up the treble?

Whenever those ten minutes in the car were over, we'd sling our backpacks over both shoulders to differentiate ourselves from the Phish heads and lacrosse players, as if there was some need to do so, and trundle off to class.

In precal, I sat between Heba Salaama and Paul Offen. Years later, Heba Salaama, better known to the greater student public as Heavy Salami, won a hundred thousand dollars on some network TV weight-loss show, but back before her dreams came true, in those pre-9/11 days when the last name Salaama was simply a curiosity, Heba was the terrifying, ethnically ambiguous girl who sat next to me in math, who kept telling me that I smelled like weed, who threatened to tell Ms. Butler if I didn't let her copy last night's homework. Paul Offen, our school's lone autistic kid, complete with an old man's gut, a greasy maw of black, thick hair, and a beard of pimples whose size and brightness were all the evidence we needed to prove God's great indifference, sat to my left. All of us who thought we were good and openhearted funneled our piteous love into Paul Offen. Girls were forever buttoning up his polo shirts to cover up his wiry black chest hairs and the sad paleness of his tits. The kids of Chapel Hill's noblest class—the beautiful interrelated kids whose parents operated on hearts and ran artists' retreats—were always driving off campus with Paul Offen riding shotgun, oblivious to how much we all secretly hated him for taking up such a coveted space.

Everyone rationalized God's cruelty by trumpeting up Paul Offen's abilities in all things math. Paul Offen, they said, had been a chess prodigy who had gone off the rails. That was what had made him autistic. Paul Offen was only in Precalculus and not BC Calculus because Mr. Thomas, the effete, dandruff-speckled head of the math department, was prejudiced. The truth, of course, was that Paul Offen was not good at math and the only reason why he passed precal was that whenever we had a test and Ms. Butler would retire behind her desk to think fondly of her husband and his hefty load of account books and calculators, she would stare at the thick-necked and charming lacrosse dudes who were taking Precalculus for their second, third time. Had she bothered to watch the row with the big Arab girl, the melon-headed Asian whose eyes were always squintier and bloodshot, and the autistic kid, she would have seen two unabashed sets of eyes planted firmly on my paper. And had Ms. Butler taught trigonometry the semester before or Algebra II before that, and if she had been the sort of louse who simply cannot gloss over God's apparent levity, then she would have known what only I knew, that Paul Offen's math genius was always in lockstep with my own. Over four straight semesters, he and I got everything right and wrong together. I think Mr. Thomas might have known because after passing back yet another test that Paul Offen and I had seen eye to eye on, he asked me to stay after class. Taking off his glasses to wipe away some of the dandruff that was always storming over his head, he asked me if I minded answering an awkward question. I have no idea what sort of look was on my face, but it must have been awful, because Mr. Thomas just sighed and told me I could go to lunch, and nobody ever spoke of it again.

Paul Offen, for his part, won the math award for our senior year. In the well-tended section of my memories, I can still remember the academic awards ceremony: the stifling heat in the gym, how it flushed the bare legs of the cheerleaders into a radiant pink, the line of teachers in modified short-sleeved black gowns, which, on account of a budget crisis, looked as if they had been made out of modified garment bags, the clatter of brass and the dull pound of the bass drum as the band shifted about in the bleachers, the hard-screwed scorn on the faces of those who were to be honored as they awaited the jeers of the mob. In earlier years, they had always ended with the English awards, but this year, because Paul Offen was being honored, the math award had been moved to the anchor position. I sat up in the bleachers by myself and watched as my Jewish friends all took their awards and quickly scuttled off stage. When Mr. Thomas walked up to the stage, the crowd fell into a hush. All you could hear were the nasty shushes from all the bighearted girls. Mr. Thomas said something about grace and diamonds in the rough, and we all grimaced, but when he finally announced Paul Offen's name, the crowd leaped to its feet, the band blew out "St. Thomas," and the gym was filled with thunderous applause. Paul Offen waddled across the stage and stood stiffly as Mr. Thomas hugged him and handed him his reward: a protractor planted on a slate mount. He looked up at us through his greasy glasses and the hedge of his thick, unruly bangs, and nothing on his face registered that this was a moment any different from any other in his life.

For years, for me, the deep-sea trough, point bottom of human sadness, existence, even, was Paul Offen not being good at math. I did not begrudge him for cheating off me, nor did I care about the math award, or even the sham of his reception. Rather, it upset me to know that the will of an entire town, all meshed together to force God's equalizing hand, could not actually make Paul Offen good at math, and, instead, it had been the stupidest and most typical of scenarios that had validated his offering to us all. Paul Offen had cheated off the Asian kid. The next year, as I was trooping around from rave to rave with Hugh, trying to kill myself in the ugliest way possible, I would sometimes stare out at the groups of kids screeching and blissfully engaging in chemical bondage and suddenly be back in that gym with the same heat, the same flushed cheerleading thighs, the same efforted and brutal love. A silly slogan would flit through my head—"It is never not Paul Offen."

Forty years after the Sumer of Love, I moved to San Francisco, because, among other things, of the Summer of Love. There was a girl back in New York who would never forgive me. And another in Boston. Both girls were of the caretaking type, and when they saw someone whose roots had been blasted up out of the ground, they tried their best to pat back down the dirt. What the Baby Molester's sister said about San Francisco is true—the worst have scraped out the mantle of the best and wear it around as something real. It takes no genius to see that. But I moved to San Francisco because the masquerade of kindly gestures is, at least, kind. And it remains kind. And all the people who would sit back and comment on the garishness of the costumes, the hollowness of the dialogue, the lack of divine conviction, well, all those people are either dead or fifteen years old.

11.   When the funeral finally broke up around dusk, what was left of the crowd stumbled back down the hill, snapping heels, rolling drums, giggling at misfortune. I was hammered. From its crest, the hill looked like a soft green slide. A few of the girls began tumbling down. All those surgically enhanced curves bouncing or not bouncing on their way to the street. I revved back, ready to launch myself after them, but then I saw Ellen's outstretched hand, palm turned up, waiting for me to accompany her down the hill.

How were we going to get back to San Francisco? Officer Bar Davis's squad car was gone. Ellen called the cab company, but they said it would be half an hour before anyone could get down to Colma. The funeral goers were piling into a fleet of unmarked white vans, and just as I was about to head over to ask if they had any room, a black limo pulled up in front of us. The window rolled down, revealing Hofspaur's cue ball head.

"I imagine you have some questions. Come on inside. We'll give you a lift back to the hotel."

BOOK SEVEN

The door of 172 Pacific was heavy, black. A Hot Topic's worth of religious trinkets had been tacked up on the white frame. There was a mezuzah, a dreamcatcher with blue threads faded from the weather, a bronzish crucifix with a nappy-headed Jesus hanging from the nails. Just to the left of the doorbell, Finch swore he spotted a smudge of blood.

After knocking, Finch went through a litany of questions, whose answers, he hoped, would help verify his sanity. What has happened today? Did these circumstances happen to you, or did you create these circumstances? Answer chronologically, please. Where the fuck is your gun?

Before he could draft any answers, the door swung open.

It was Bad Vibes Bob. Finch almost didn't recognize him out of his wet suit, but there were the burlish, Popeye forearms, the marine chin, the bright blue eyes, which might have been even beautiful had they not been sold off, soul and all, into the slavery of scorn. For a moment, the two men stared at one another in the doorway. Finch, poker-faced, coppish; Bad Vibes Bob seething, but not with anything more than the usual bad vibes.

Bad Vibes Bob broke the silence. "What's up, dude."

"Can I talk to you?"

"Yeah." Bad Vibes Bob turned his back and slouched off into the dark foyer. Over his shoulder, he said, "Come on in. We were wondering when you guys would show up."

172 Pacific was in dire need of a woman's touch. Finch felt his nose wrinkling at the bare white walls, the cracked cornices and moldings, the scatter of empties, loose pretzels, the bags and fry containers from Burger King, McDonald's, Wendy's, Carl's Jr.

Finch muttered, "Where is there a Wendy's in this city?"

Bad Vibes said, "Daly City. On the way back from Lindy."

"You surf Lindy now?"

"I did three weeks ago. South winds."

"You're going all soft on us, Bob."

In the kitchen, a pyramid of pizza boxes was stacked up on the island. Everything smelled like trash after a heavy rain. Through some unseen speaker, Finch heard the crescendoing chorus of "Take on Me." The doors of the cabinets had all been ripped off. An army of plastic figurines, most still in their original boxes, stared down from the shelves. Finch could feel their menace. At the back of the kitchen, at a table crammed with CD cases and computer monitors, sat the fattest man

Finch had ever seen in his life. Some striped, yellow thing sat atop his mountainous gut. The fat man was stroking this thing's head, but his attention was riveted on the screens. He did not look up when Finch and Bad Vibes Bob entered the kitchen, nor did he look up when the yellow thing hopped off his gut and scampered over to Bad Vibes Bob. Only when "Take on Me" finally wound itself out did the fat man look up at Finch with two unblinking and noncommittal troll eyes, staring through Coke-bottle glasses. The glare from the monitor contoured the whorls of grease on the lenses, the matting of sweat on his forehead, and the two-day growth on his chin, sparse and black.

Finch regretted not bringing his gun to the party. The fat man fanned out his monitors invitingly and said, "Hello. Welcome, Inspector Finch. We have something to show you."

That was when Heather stepped into the kitchen. With Finch's gun, of course.

Before Finch could envision what might go down, Heather just up and fired.

GOOD-TIME SLIM, UNCLE DOOBIE, AND THE GREAT FRISCO FREAK-OUT

1. The limo was a relic. The champagne glasses were from the Gordon Gekko collection, the mini-TV in the corner looked as if it should be ticking off skyrocketing stock quotes for Wang Computers. I felt a bit embarrassed for us all, driving around in this elongated heap of anachronisms. But a limo is still a limo, I guess.

When we turned onto the highway, Hofspaur hit a button and the glass partition slid down, revealing the same short-cropped, blond head of hair we had seen from the backseat of Officer Bar Davis's squad car.

She turned around and winced.

Hofspaur said, "You two have already met Field Agent Bernstein."

Ellen coughed. Me, I was too drunk. Field Agent Bernstein, née Officer Bar Davis, jerked the wheel, swerving the limo through two lanes of traffic, onto the exit ramp for the 1 South. "We have to be careful that we're not followed." Hofspaur explained, "You two are in some danger, and it's paramount we reach a safe space. From here on out, please maintain radio silence. Cell phones off."

We drove down the hill toward Pacifica through a bank head of thick, gray fog. In the parking lot of a McDonald's, Field Agent Bernstein herded us out of the limo and into a green Toyota Corolla. We drove around on the surface streets, passing by squat, efficient houses whose bright colors and well-tended lawns couldn't quite ward off the fog's cold grip. At the corner of some street and another, a cavalry of teenage kids rode by on BMX bikes that had been rigged up with surfboard racks. Their wet suits were draped, like black flags, over their handlebars. We pulled up in front of a nondescript pink house and watched as the fog slowly erased their retreating forms.

Field Agent Bernstein got out of the car and started walking up toward the pink house. Hofspaur said, "Come along."

We did, although now that I think about it, I have no idea why.

FOR THE ENTIRETY of our silent drive down the 1, the same two scenes kept running through my head. In the first, I was dying somewhere squalid with a bullet in my gut. As I gasped for air and muttered some meaningful stuff, Ellen's face would hover over me like some radiant, teary planet. She would press her finger to my lips and say, "I have to say something," and then confess, earnestly, that she was a double agent working for someone or the other. "But," she would say as I was gathering up my last breath, "somewhere along the way, I fell in love and I'm sorry."

In the second scenario, Ellen lies dying on some squalid floor and I am the one hovering like some radiant, teary planet, but this time, when she makes her gasping, tortured confession, she reveals her pregnancy.

I know it was ridiculous, but try to understand, it had just dawned on me that I barely knew this girl. If Bar Davis was not Bar Davis and our danger was not danger, wasn't it also possible that Ellen was not Ellen? But there was nothing to do. I took her wrist and led her into the pink house.

2 . Inside, the furniture was old. The television was huge. The photos stared out from thick bronze frames. An antique foggy mirror hung from its mount—all the evidence of an old woman who, from time to time, receives gifts from her offspring. Bar Davis was seated on a couch next to Hofspaur, still grimacing, but it was more of a grimace of soft concern, the way a dog lover will grimace as he clips the toenails of his beloved golden. She waved toward a yellow cretonne settee and said, "Please. Sit down and listen.

"As Miles alluded to before, I have not been completely forth-right about my identity, so allow me to reintroduce myself. My name is Tovah Bernstein of the Federal Bureau of Investigation. Recently, I have come across some information that should be concerning to both of you, but especially Mister Kim. Without going into unnecessary detail, Mr. Kim, we have reason to believe that members of the San Francisco Police Department, acting under the command of an executive at a large Internet security company, have enacted a plot to frame you for the murders of your former neighbor, Miss Dolores Stone, and your former colleague, Mister William Curren.

"Last night, however, as you might have heard on the news, a letter was received from a group calling themselves the Brownstone Knights.

The letter was mostly incomprehensible, but thanks to the efforts of Inspector James Kim, the origin of the Brownstone Knights was quickly traced back to the writings of Cho Seung-Hui.

"The confluence of the fact that you were the only person connected to both victims and your own peculiar background, which includes both Korean heritage and a laundry list of published short stories, all of which, I might add, exhibit a fascination with guns, gang culture, physical abuse, and violence—"

I interrupted her. "What?"

"What to what?"

"Published short stories? Gang culture? Physical abuse?"

"Are you denying this?"

"I've published one story. It was about a retard and his brother. And it didn't even count because they didn't pay me."

I squeezed Ellen's hand.

"I see." Reaching into the slash pocket of her blazer, she produced a folded sheet of paper. "You are not the author of 'Rapey Time Militia,' 'Tonz of Gunz,' 'Mrs. Brownstone,' and 'Cunty Kinte and the Last Molester,' all published in *Ammo* and *Pussy Quarterly Review*?"

"Wikipedia?"

"What?"

"Those stories, you found them on my Wikipedia page, right?"

Ellen broke her silence. She asked, "You have a Wikipedia page?"

"My friend Adam made a Wikipedia page for me when we were in graduate school. It was a joke. None of those stories are real. I've just never bothered to take it down because what's the point?"

"Could you please explain this, then?"

She reached back into the same pocket and pulled out a thick, folded square of paper. Printed across the top, in big bold letters, was the title "Cunty Kinte and the Last Molester." The first sentence read, "When Cunty Kinte was born, his father took him to the soothsayer, who placed the young boy in a bed of tea leaves and molested him."

"I didn't write this. I never write in the third person."

"It's possible it was planted online."

"Why?"

"Because with this evidence, Mister Kim, and your general antisocial tendencies, a convincing story will be told to the general public that pits you as a menace against the greater society."

"What?"

"Yes. The organization behind these actions is BFG, a Silicon Valley Internet security company. Now that people's bank accounts and children are relatively safe, this company has decided to branch out into a different sort of security, namely, protecting people's online identities from predators such as yourself. Every time a white person gets killed now, this company, through a network of hyperlocal blogs and news organizations, tries to link the victim and the killer through a form of social media. By taking the randomness out of every murder, they create monsters and put them right under your bed."

"But I didn't kill anyone."

"We understand that now."

"So, uh, what's going on?"

"What we do know, Mister Kim, is that you, I'm sorry to say, make a pretty scary monster."

In the haze brought on by this erratic panic and eight Cape Codders,

I thought she was calling me pretty. But then I looked into the gilt, smoky mirror and saw the truth. At least, I thought, Ellen looked nice in that fucked-up hat.

"You, with your tony educational background, your ethnic background, which links you to the Virginia Tech killings, and your prolific presence on the Internet, are the new breed of monster."

"Really." Despite everything, I was still somehow flattered.

"I do not know what they will do from here on out, but I would not be surprised if more of these sorts of stories, authored by you, began appearing in far-off stretches of the Internet. The story will be the same. You are a frustrated young writer living in the serial killer capital of America, who, on several occasions, has posted ironical things about Cho Seung-Hui. They will find what I found quite easily—the rap lyrics posted on Internet forums, the disturbingly violent short stories, the history of fights in college, the rampant drug use. There will be interviews with kids from your high school who will say you were bullied and made to feel inferior. They will interview your ex-girlfriends, who, no matter what they say, will be white. Are you understanding me?"

"Yes. I mean except the white girlfriend part."

"Well, that's less important."

"Okay, then."

She paused, mercifully, and smoothed out the front of her skirt. Ellen, I noticed, was crying again. Hofspaur, elbows on knees, emanated a Buddha-like calm, as if all of this was just another example of whatever this was an example of. I couldn't help but think he was right.

Tovah Bernstein asked, "Do you want to know why I'm telling you this?"

"Sure. I don't care."

"Because your last victim, Philip, is you."

3.   Like all moody, hell-bent children, I grew up knowing I was not long for this earth. I remember lying in bed at night, trying to imagine a saggier, wiser me. When I succeeded in projecting a bowlarama gut, my face would still be my face. If I scrolled up to edit the face, the gut would shrivel back into my fifteen-year-old stomach. My cock hung down lower in these imaginings (gravity's inevitable favor), but my legs would lose their manly hair. A totality of vision was always out of reach. This incompleteness sieved out my faith for a future like the futures of others.

It's fair to point out: I wasn't really trying.

This condition, I'll call it, has never been addressed, but over the years, the demands of staying alive have wrested away the edges of incompleteness and roughly stitched them together. I have stopped worrying about my inability to imagine myself as an older man, but in doing so, I warped what I had counted on as being good, my quick-flamed glory. The need to find girls to share my bed, the need to see myself as a social being, the need to avoid adverbs, the need to win at chess, Scrabble, crossword puzzles, the need to not be moody and the need to be moody provided a wearable shield against the darkness, but they never could quite convince me that I should still be existing anymore.

When Field Agent Tovah Bernstein announced my imminent death, the stitches hemming in my imagined life split. The lumpy tapestry spread out, revealing its blackening gaps. As I looked up at the march of truncated and half-formed bodies, my stowed-away celluloid places and their associated place names, I was inundated with something much better than relief. There I was, headless, save a floating mop of graying hair, walking down some street. The buildings on either side made no sense—there was the communist ice cream shop on the corner of 18th and Guerrero, the red awning of a pizza slice counter on 110th and Broadway, my high school's vocational building, spare, squat, and brick, the used book store in Chapel Hill where I had spent my allowance, dutifully building up a library that might match my towering intellectual vanity. And there was Ellen, accompanying me through this maze of associations, her face blurry, her legs thick and sturdy. I could see a Christmas card of our children in Santa hats—the only one who looked at all like me was grimacing. There we were in some overgrown marshland, surrounded by cattails, staring up at the white plume of the *Challenger* traced out across the murky blue sky. There we were, standing by the leaded windows of our classic six on Riverside Drive, a few blocks too far up to truly still be called Riverside Drive, watching as a mob of zombies thunked their rotting fists against the front door of our building. There, surrounded by blue-green landscapes and whorls of qi lines, we sat in a noodle shop in Seoul, my mother's apparition hovering nearby. Through the paper walls, we heard her tell us about how, before she ever met my father, he used to come down to this noodle shop to study, and how she will always return to sit in this booth with a view of the street, to pick at the cheap chajangmyun, because even when you fall out of love with someone, you are still in love with who they were before they met you.

Relief flooded out of my fingertips. I hiccuped.

You please believe. I did not want this to become a love story. Were the circumstances different, I would have been embarrassed to know that so much was contingent on this girl I barely knew. But Field Agent Tovah Bernstein had laid out a potential escape, a way to dive right into the darkness, and although the iterations of self on the cloth were all headless, monstrous, moaning, all the Ellens were clearer, somehow.

I felt something familiar spark up, tinder, and ignite.

I asked, "Where the fuck are these people?"

BOOK EIGHT

The shot hit the fat man in the shoulder. He grunted, blinked a dozen times, keeled over. Finch dived behind the island, landing squarely on the back of the fat, striped yellow thing. From under the island, he could see Bad Vibes Bob's scuffed Doc Martens planted firmly on the tile. Somebody was saying something to somebody, and the fat yellow thing was squealing and squirming under his chest. The nitrous whonging returned. Finch's vision grayed at the edges.

A weight pressed down on the back of his neck. A cell phone clattered on the tile near Finch's head.

"Please don't struggle, Sidney. This has very little to do with you. Now please, call an ambulance for our fat friend."

GUN IN RIBS, Finch drove the Subaru down toward the Mission. Bad Vibes Bob was laid out in the backseat, his wrists zip tied behind his back. He was cursing, but without much conviction. At the intersection of 20th and Mission, Lionface instructed Finch to park in front of the old Victoria Theatre sign. Rusted out and long since gutted of its lights, the Victoria sign stuck up over the storefronts, a bit of Coney Island shipped out to San Francisco. Two men jogged over and positioned themselves on either side of the Subaru. The one on Finch's side pulled up his shirt, revealing a gun butt stuck in the waist of his pants.

Lionface said, "We are going into this club to watch this show. Don't ask why. Just know that there are at least thirty men in there just like these men. Their only job is to watch over you. If you do not want bullets to fly in a club, I would suggest you remain calm and listen to all of my instructions. Again, there is no need for all of this to get ugly. At the end, I promise to explain. Now please, get out and these men will escort you quietly to your reserved seats."

The man on Finch's side tapped on the window.

NERDS SWARMED THE 12 Galaxies. Standing at the threshold, Finch stared out at all the milling children. Once again, he hated them. He wished Sarah could be the one with the gun up in his back, so that she might say something damning about the postcollegiate population of San Francisco: how poorly they dress, how behind Brooklyn, how earnest their art, how boring and consuming their jobs down in Silicon Valley, how organic scam, their organic chard.

As for the gun in his back, Finch had no opinion, but as he edged and apologized his way through the crowd, he felt the bump of the joy he had felt outside of the bakery in Pescadero. He couldn't quite draw the exact line back to some earlier happy memory and haul himself back toward it, but he knew, just by the totality of the joy, that this time it had something to do with his memory of Sarah.

Where was she? And just how beautifully would she have hated what was here?

At the back of the club, near the stage, were five rows of folding chairs, each one occupied, save the two at the stage-left end of the front row. Finch, who, like all surfers, made a habit of examining the bodies of other built men to ferret out whether the muscles were produced by labor and nature, or by the unnatural efficiency of machines and gyms, noticed that the heavy's smooth skin and evenly proportioned arms screamed of gym strength, which meant he, Finch, who had built his strength both in academy training and in the stormy waters of Ocean Beach, had little to fear. He exhaled, cracked a baffling smile at his captor, and, with the joy still knocking about his ribs, Inspector Sid "Keanu" Finch sat down.

ON STAGE, FIVE production assistants hopped about like ravens at a picnic, adjusting this, rolling that over there, and generally looking pleased with the impossibility of how busy they were. The floodlights above the stage had not been turned on yet, but on the black backdrop, Finch could see the flickering, probably on purpose, projected image of an Asian man in a beat suit trudging through Willie Mays Plaza, placard on shoulder. He, native San Franciscan, or, as the OB locals liked to say, Real Live Salty Fuck, of course recognized Frank Chu. Spinning around the video feed were uncommon fonts in Frank Chu's preferred colors—magenta, baby blue, lavender, and fire engine red—spelling out all the words that only made sense to Chu and the ever-expanding eighteen thousand galaxy illuminati, led by President Bill Clinton, who controlled the rights to his reality TV show.

ULTIMATE: ZEGNATROCICED:

ANALYSISED: COMPLIMENTARY FREE BUDWEISERS: MENARD:

TECNITRONICED: ROSSINIALIZED: SEXTROLOGICALLED:

INTERRED-GALATIALLED: OMEGATRONICED: RETORICALLED:

TUTRALOGICALLED: ESCALAED: BETATRONICED: RELEVANT:

CIRCUM-QUADROLOGICALLED:

DEPOSITIONS: ALTRALOGICALLED: INSTANTANEOUSED:

DECKED-TRONICED: IMPEACH CLINTON: IMPEACH CLINTON:

IMPEACH CLINTON: CAMERON: KOTSRDODENIKEL EMANATIONS:

TOSS: GUTSPROSENICAL COVERAGE: PHIXGRSTRENIKUL:

APOLOGETICS: EMBELLISHMENTS COSOLATIONS:

ERGOFRENICUL EMBRYONIC: PBS: NOLTSGROGRENICOL

COVERAGE: UTRDRENIKAL: ANTITHESIS

INCENTIVIEZEZ: CHROMOGENIC:

CLEVERLY: STATUTORY SYNCHING: ARGITHENICAL:

475,000 GALAXIES

Like anyone who works downtown, Finch had had his share of run-ins with Frank Chu, usually at the ballpark, but had never thought much of him. Once, while driving around aimlessly with Kim, he had almost run Frank Chu over at a crosswalk. When he rolled down the window to apologize, expecting a salvo of angry insanity, Frank Chu had simply said, "Hello, Officer," before shuffling over to the other side of the road. Kim had said, "I'm glad that guy's Chinese."

When the video feed of Frank Chu by the ballpark ended, another, much grainier, washed-out scene kicked up, this one showing a wiry black man standing on the steps of a squat, modern, thoroughly concrete building. Despite having never seen the building in person, Finch could tell, somehow, that this was Berkeley, and, from the evocation of imprecise, blurry colors, thinly cut slacks, and big hair, he deduced that whatever was about to happen probably happened back in the seventies. For a minute or so, the man simply stood at the top of the steps, watching disinterestedly as a steady parade of young faces filed on by. Then, with a whoop, unheard, but signaled by his gaping mouth, he hopped onto a bronze guide rail and slid down, arms outstretched, hopping off at the last possible moment and disappearing off the bottom of the frame. As with the video of Frank Chu, a constellation of words surrounded this video, but they had been clustered into short slogans, which, if properly situated, might have passed off as poetic.

> We are THE ONE. Struggles are struggles. Beware the
> limping men. Wisdom is just we's dumb to me. Am I here for
> the cause, or just because? We shall overcum. Cork the pork
> cause I digs the pigs. Somebody Blew up America. The God of
> Love is Dead but the God of War, he lives on. Respect kills
> the talk. Be celestial in the body, celestial in the mind.

Each video had been about a minute in length, but to Finch, time had stalled. He had already dismissed the notion that he was in much danger.

All of it—the heavy, who, at regular intervals, was still jabbing the barrel of his gun into Finch's ribs, the kids scurrying up on stage, the merch stand selling black T-shirts with Frank Chu words printed across the front, the gangly kids, their Western shirts, their cheap domestic beers, their cuffed jeans, all of it some coy reference back to an irretrievable past when America would not have tolerated their gluttony—seemed very funny to Finch.

The heavy, distressed, flashed a hand sign that Finch recognized as the calling card of the Mara Salvatrucha 13. Finch laughed, again.

Lionface's breasts, covered by a Zengatronic T-shirt, but still unmistakably hers, appeared in front of him. She sat down in his lap and pressed her mouth to his ear. He felt her sculpted flanks shift menacingly up against his crotch. In a hissing, slow voice, she said, "Listen. There are twenty-five men in this place who are carrying weapons. Each one has been instructed to shoot to kill. You have no fucking clue what is going on, but if you want to stay alive, you had better shut the fuck up, sit quietly, and do everything I tell you to do. This is not a joke."

"Eh."

"Eh? Take a look back at the bar. See how 'eh' this is about to get."

Finch complied. Sitting by the bar, swarmed by kids in black shirts, he spotted a tiny, mottled potato head. His heart leapt.

LEPER IN THE BACKFIELD

1. And so we found ourselves at the 12 Galaxies. Field Agent Tovah Bernstein, née Officer Bar Davis, had given each of us a pager. When trouble comes, she said, press the red button. She promised her team would provide a swift response.

Who was this team? The bar was overrun with its usual crowd of dudes in their mid-thirties, each one aging catastrophically—spare tires tucked into tight V-neck shirts, horn-rimmed glasses, lenses greased up by the usual straggle of thin, long hair, a feigned earnestness, referential fucking humor—a cabal of high school girls forever updating and reupdating the parlor scenes from *Little Women*.

Also, I admit it: Carrying a gun is nice. Each time the holster banged against my chest, it felt like a bionic heartbeat. Ellen had stowed her gun in her handbag, reasoning that if there was a need to shoot, I should be the one to pull the trigger. How grateful I was to hear that! Till then, I had simply assumed that she, athlete supreme, feminist by bodily example, and recipient of better alumni magazines, would have taken the lead.

2. The lights dimmed. The crowd shuffled up toward the stage. I looked over at Ellen. She just shook her head.

A thin man trudged onto the stage. From our spot back at the bar, all I could make out was the flash of a large pink birthmark on his cheek. I can't remember if it was the left or right cheek. When his somber march to the microphone stand came to its end, he about-faced and said, "Thank you guys for coming out to the party. We have two wonderful performers tonight, including the man, the legend, Frank Chu. Afterward, myself and Alan, my co-owner over the years, will be saying some words for the closing of the club. But before all that tearful sadness, let's celebrate what made the 12 Galaxies a Mission staple since 2002. Our great performers. So, first let's welcome Mr. Brownstone to the stage."

The black curtain behind the stage ruffled and split. Out came James, naked, save a codpiece and Ellen's teal shoes. Pigeon-toed, ankles collapsing from the effort, he strutted up to the mike.

"Hello, everybody. Thank you so much for coming out tonight. You could've been anywhere, but you're here with me, and I thank you. We have a great show for you tonight. Frank Chu is here. Thank you so much. I am Mr. Brownstone, your host for the festivities, and I'd like to get you warmed up with a little of what I call . . . po-eh-tree!"

From speakers hanging over the stage, a trio of voices sang out an unmistakable gospel harmony: "Well Mary, Mary don't you weep . . . Tell Martha not to moan . . . Martha don't you moan. Pharaoh's army . . . Pharaoh's army . . . know they've been drowned in the Red Sea . . . Singing, Mary . . . oh Mary don't you weep . . . Tell Martha not to moan . . . Moh-whoawhoawhoa-an . . ."

The familiarity of the hymn, the gospel chords unmistakable from

Mahalia Jackson YouTube searches, *Ray*, and all those civil rights videos watched to kill time in elementary school Februaries, sent a charge through the crowd. Cell phones and flipcams were glowing.

I'm proud to say, I knew better. Because when the gospel trio got to the second "Martha don't you moan," the alto collapsed down into a flat, souring the harmony into something else, a chord I had heard hundreds of times before in Seth's orange Volvo.

James, thank God, complied.

"Bonebonebonebone . . . bone . . . bone, bone, bone. Bonebonebonebonebone . . . bone . . . bone, bone, bone, bone! Now tell me what ya gonna do, where there ain't nowhere to run. . . . When judgment comes for you, when judgment comes for you! What you gonna do, when there ain't nowhere to hide, when judgment comes for you, 'cause it's gonna come. . . ."

I heard Ellen gasp, and sweet relief washed over me again. She knew. Swelling in a pause, James threw up his hands in a maestro's pose and waited as the crowd took in a deep breath, ready to sing along.

"Ehhh*son*, liggimowahlay, easyseemichar-LAY, lilboogodogogotay, and I'm gonna miss everybody, ImaohnahrohwiBomagawhatheyloay . . . wheplaywidestinadee fometosay . . . duhdoomackasaylillazykaymay, todlmayseewell*Bury Me*myGan-Ganandhwenyoucaaaayn. . . ."

DURING ONE OF those mornings in the orange Volvo, when we were feeling wild enough to skip precalculus, Seth and I tried to transcribe every word in *E. 1999 Eternal.* How could we have known, back then, how much damage we were doing to our future selves? Because every time "Tha Crossroads" comes on, everyone, well, everyone I know, at least, starts singing along incoherently, but smiling, and I, who know the actual words, feel cheated, at least a bit, because there are only so many songs a bunch of kids who grew up together can sing together without feeling territorial, nasty, or horny, and when these moments come unforced, it's nice to be thinking the same things as everyone else.

I understand. I am being insufferable. It has occurred to me several times over the years to just go ahead and fake it. Mumble along with the crowd and hit the only distinguishable parts that everyone knows—"can anyone anybody tell me why? We die, we die, we die . . ."—and the unmistakable, feet-splitting "And I miss my uncle George."

And yet, Ellen's radiant face, a swimming pool at night, the kids stomping around, incoherently babbling along to this song, which could have been about anything, really (how would anyone know?), but, by dint of the music video, which featured some overly lit, dry-ice-choked stage on which the five Bone Thugs, solemn angels, clasped their hands, and pleaded for the Angel of Death to not take away their friends, that we all knew was about death, and not our deaths, but a scattershot brand whose quickness we would never quite comprehend, and, of course, the understanding that my days on earth might end tonight, all of it, dare I say, the synthesis of these melancholy, conditional thoughts, opened up a battered vault of nostalgia.

I staggered a bit. I thought of Ronizm, Bone Thugs, quesadillas in plastic bags. For some reason, I felt very sad about my sister. Once all this was over, I was going to give her a call.

JAMES HOBBLED OFFSTAGE to riotous applause. A woman sidled up next to me at the bar. Her breasts were bundled up in a T-shirt that read ZENGATRONIC.

This Zengatronic smiled. She said, "James told me to tell you that he apologizes for stealing your girlfriend's shoes, and if you come backstage, he will both return the shoes and reimburse the cost. Please follow me."

I reached into my pocket and hit the button of my pager. I saw Ellen do the same. Then, up near the stage, at the end of the front row of folding chairs, a head, hair grease shining in the floodlight, popped to attention.

BOOK NINE

T h e heavy bolted upright, reached beneath the lapel of his leather overcoat. Steeling himself for the sight of a gun, Finch held his breath, clenched his pecs, anticipating whatever takedown he would have to employ. But the heavy only pulled out a pager, clicked it a couple of times, grunted, and settled back into his seat.

Mr. Brownstone's performance had sprayed a viscous satisfaction over the crowd. Everyone was smiling wanly at one another, faces glistening, happy to share in the melancholy connection found only when we sing childhood songs with strangers. Especially sad, silly songs. Finch, thirty-nine in August, had never heard "Tha Crossroads" before, but even he, forever cynic, now hardened to a seemingly impending death, could feel the joy knocking around his chest reach its tendrils out and join hands with these sappy children.

The heavy, he noticed, had craned his neck to look back at the bar, where Lionface was talking to some Asian kid in a power tie and a sturdy-looking girl whose vintage dress and hat could not quite cover up the fact that she belonged somewhere in the Marina. But before he could speculate on the identity, or, perhaps, utility of the two costumed kids, the lights dimmed.

Followed by a lone spotlight, Frank Chu trudged up the steps to the stage. Someone had put him in a beige suit, but it wore badly, loose in the ass and shoulders, dragging at the cuffs. Sweat glistened off his brow, and even from his seat, Finch could smell the unmistakable pungency of ginseng root or ginkgo leaf or one of those mediciney smells that, along with rotting fish and edible frogs swimming in kiddie pools, turn every Chinatown into a summertime horror show. At least for most of us.

His tortoiseshell sunglasses hung low on his nose, but even their opulence, squared off and clearly of the right brand, could not cover the deep lines that creased his cheeks, the gristly fat that hung down from his chin. Tightly gripped in his right hand, dented and sweating, was a can of Budweiser. Without his sign, which stood propped up against the bar, he could have been any half-cocked Chinese grandfather in any of the karaoke bars on Geary or down on Jackson, ready to sing a ballad to God knows what, probably a cherry blossom, in the preferred Chinese guttural baritone.

Good Lord, Finch thought to himself, Frank Chu looks old.

Maybe it was the oppression of the spotlight, but as Frank Chu stood at the mike, soaking in the whoops from the crowd, blinking against the flashes of the digital cameras, he cowered a bit. After the hoots and catcalls died down, he adjusted the mike stand down, and began his raspy, rhythmic speech.

"I am glad, ah, you are all here to support, ah, my fight against the 12 Galaxies, ah, and their treasons and perversions against humanity, this is a kind place where they have given me many things like checks for one hundred dollars for advertising, ah, their bar on the back of my sign and many free complimentary Budweisers. For many years, the 12 Galaxies, ah, controlling their hurricane devices, ah, have committed war crimes against humanity, ah, like turning on their wind machines, ah, to drown the population of New Orleans because of their ancestries. The 12 Galaxies have continually withheld payment from me and my family, led by President Bill Clinton, he and the 12 Galaxies have withheld payment as they, ah, turned us into movie stars, ah, and we have support of many movie stars, ah, and they agree the 12 Galaxies must pay."

A cheer rattled through the crowd. Even the heavy managed a slow clap.

"It is the sum of three point five billion dollars, and for many years, I have notified the authorities of this injustice done to me and my family. In 1998, the *San Francisco Chronicle* wrote a cover piece on my protests, bringing to light the injustice done to me and my family by the 12 Galaxies, who have withheld payment for many years. I thank them for their help. In 2001, the *San Francisco Examiner* named me the city's best protester, and I thank them for helping me expose the battle between the eighteen thousand galaxies and the 12 Galaxies. But tonight is about the 12 Galaxies nightclub, which, for many years, has supported me with checks for a hundred dollars and many free complimentary Budweisers. In 2002, the club opened to help me expose the 12 Galaxies and reclaim the three point five billion dollars owed to me by President Bill Clinton."

Someone yelled, "Impeach Clinton!" Frank Chu grimaced.

Finch had no real opinion on that. He looked back at the bar, but Lionface and the kids were gone.

Instead, he opened up his cell phone and stared in again at the image of Sarah's hairy bush. The heavy grunted, tried to slap away the phone. In one quick motion, Finch lifted up his shirt and pulled down the waist of his pants, exposing an inch of pubes and the remains of what had once been a ripping six-pack. He snapped a photo. Smoky, dark, and badly pixelated, the photo made his pubes looked like mold creepers, but the shadowy effect had restored his six-pack to some of its prior glory. Finch typed, "LET'S COMPARE???"

The heavy jammed something into Finch's ribs. It was probably a gun.

Finch hit SEND.

SORRY, WRONG CLOSET

Z e n g a t r o n i c led us through the crowd, past the stage, up to a blacked-out door. Again, I pressed the pager. Again, the thick-necked Guido type in the front row started upright. Sitting next to him was some older guy who reeked of half-formed, if not fetal, authority. Were these our saviors? I tried to make eye contact, but then thought better of it. Zengatronic knocked on the door and then turned to us. Her mouth stretched out into a receptionist's tight smile. Ellen, hyperventilating, opened up her handbag. For a second, I thought she might puke right in there, but then I remembered.

The gun.

The door swung open.

Before committing myself, or us, rather, to whatever was beyond that door, I looked back at the crowd for Tovah Bernstein's bleach-blond hair. There it was, just one row back, incandescent in the dimming overhead lights. Not indelicately, she leaned her head out into the aisle, looked me straight in the eye, and nodded.

Okay.

THE BACKSTAGE AREA at the 12 Galaxies was just a well-stocked utility closet with a few beat-up couches pushed up against the wall, and a coffee table, dorm-issue, stacked up high with alternative weeklies and pizza boxes. James was plopped down on one of the couches. He motioned for us to do the same. Zengatronic closed the door and leaned up against a rusty cylindrical boiler.

Through the wall, we could hear the crowd cheer, and then a raspy, muted voice on the PA. James, for his part, looked confused.

What a horrible place to die, I thought.

I heard a bang, a thud, the clang of metal.

I looked over.

There, by the boiler, alone, my unstoppable girlfriend lay with her hands clutched over her stomach. She looked confused as blood spurted between her fingers and onto the cement.

Zengatronic pointed the gun at my chest. She said, "It's your turn now, Mr. Brownstone."

Who was she talking to?

On cue, James stood up, reached under the couch, pulled out two Uzis, and ran through the door.

BOOK TEN

Frank Chu trudged back down the steps, where he was greeted by a crowd of autograph seekers who had printed out facsimiles of his signs. Finch felt the nudge of the heavy's gun against his ribs. Leaning over, he hissed in Finch's violated ear, "Stay cool. Stay real cool. What's about to happen is part of a show, got it?"

The spotlight, Finch saw, had come to rest on the velvety black curtain behind the stage. As the music kicked back up, the curtain ruffled and then split. Mr. Brownstone ran out onto the stage with an Uzi in each hand, screaming something in Chinese or some Asian language.

Then, guns pointed straight in the air, Mr. Brownstone began to fire away.

EVERYTHING MOVED IN such slow motion that Finch even had the time to think, Wow, the reports are right, things *do* move in slow motion. The chunks of plaster shot out of the ceiling looked as if they were falling through water, the screams of the crowd registered in a palm-dragged baritone. When the heavy grabbed Finch by the collar of his shirt, he could feel each muscle in the heavy's fingers, could sense the tightening of his forearm, the surge of power gathering in his haunches. The crowd did what crowds are supposed to do in these scenes—they ran.

Finch knew, albeit abstractly, that he was also screaming and cowering, but he could also feel, at least somewhere in his body, an unctuous disbelief over what was going on. As the heavy dragged him by his collar toward an unmarked door behind the stage, he could still assess the lack of any real danger. Sure, there was an insane man on stage firing off two Uzis, but Mr. Brownstone kept the barrels raised high, and although the chaos made it impossible to be sure, after the first few rounds, which had brought down the ceiling, Finch was sure, 51 percent sure, that Mr. Brownstone had switched over to blanks.

But before he could confirm any of this, the heavy dragged him up to a metal door and started knocking.

THE COMPUTER WORE PUKA SHELLS

D o you remember when Chris Rock was talking about Columbine and asked, "Whatever happened to crazy?" He was right, of course. The attempts to psychologically or sociologically or spiritually explain the massacre arose—with a grim, zombie hunger—out of the graves of our Protestant work ethic. Because we knew we were somehow to blame, we felt the need to work toward some absolution, to find the cure. (The use of the collective pronoun here could be read however you'd like, but I'd prefer you be generous.) When the usual viruses were rounded up, the public (again, be generous) let loose an exhausted sigh. Chris Rock's question was our panacea, the mantra we could all chant to convince ourselves of what was true—sometimes people, even kids, go crazy and kill a bunch of other people, even kids.

I mention it because I am thinking again about Cho Seung-Hui and why I have never been able to cast him off with a nice, measured "Whatever happened to crazy?" The reasons are obvious, but just as we can no longer think about Columbine without routing it through Chris

Rock's question, I, specifically, can no longer process anger without routing it through Cho Seung-Hui.

Hyung-Jae said something about it once. We were back in that soggy bar around Columbia, and we were making jokes about Cho Seung-Hui again. It was late. The Yankees were playing in Seattle. We watched a few innings, made more bad jokes. At some point, Ichiro Suzuki came up to the plate and slapped his eight billionth single of the year. Hyung Jae said, "If that Jap has inspired gooky kids in America to think, 'Hey, I can drag this tiny dick onto a baseball field and slap singles around the infield,' then Cho is like Super Ichiro because he allowed every angry Asian kid in this country whose dad sucks or who is taking shit at school or who is getting no pussy to just go ahead and think, 'Hey, I actually can shoot all these motherfuckers.'"

We both laughed because it was true. Then he asked, "Isn't some part of you a little bit proud over Cho?"

IF I TOLD you my answer, would you believe that as I stood over Ellen's quaking body, gun in hands, I, hipster dinosaur, was ready to shoot Zengatronic down?

There was a knocking at the door. Zengatronic reached down for the doorknob.

The door flew open. I shut my eyes and fired. Six or seven times.

BOOK ELEVEN

The first bullet hit Finch in the left shoulder. The second split his clavicle ridge and exited a half inch from his spine. The third hit him in the right thigh, shattering his femur. The fourth missed. The fifth missed. The sixth hit the heel of his left loafer. The seventh missed. The eighth missed.

Of course, Finch thought, of course. But other than the bullets, he couldn't quite figure out what was so goddamn obvious.

DIG YOUR OWN GRAVE AND SAVE

who knew that shooting blindly was so easy?

BOOK TWELVE

Until it happens, every cop spends an unhealthy amount of time wondering what it feels like to get shot. Cynic Finch had always assumed that it wouldn't hurt as much as it should, at least not at first. Nothing was numb, nothing was in shock. Instead, he could feel the bullet lodged in his shoulder, the one now floating in the back of his shattered thigh. If he had been able to close his eyes, he was sure he would have been able to see the slugs, the rifling on their sides, their heads, split open like mouths, calling out, feebly, their caliber.

He drifted off. As his brain drained itself of thought, the fish wriggled free and swam off. Had he had his faculties intact, Finch would have noticed, with pride, hopefully, that the only words remaining—the raised

Atlantis, dead, perhaps, but still urn burial—came from one Sullivan Ballou, a Union Army major who had died at Bull Run. On the night before the battle, Ballou had written a letter to his wife about his duty to serve his country and how it might conflict with, truncate his love for his wife and family. Finch, like everyone else, had come across the letter in Ken Burns's Civil War documentary.

Eyelids flitting, vision narrowed, Finch could hear the unmistakable, lilting fiddle refrain that had accompanied the reading of Ballou's letter. For the first time in years, he recalled standing with Sarah on the edge of the cliffs at Montara State Beach. He had just accepted his position within the homicide division. Sarah was wary of the long hours, the stress it might put on their young marriage. By way of rebuttal, Finch had memorized the entirety of Ballou's letter. At Montara, backed by ten thousand yellow wildflowers, the unruly Pacific crashing below, he had recited the letter to her.

Now, shot four times and bleeding out in a storage closet, Finch felt no shame over the crudeness of his own farewell address. He only wished he had taken a better photo. As his eyes began to shut down, he felt a buzzing against his thigh. The elegant fiddle refrain was interrupted by a two-toned chime.

A text message had arrived.

Then Siddhartha "Keanu" Finch blacked out.

SMOKE YOURSELF THIN!

I looked at my gun. And although I certainly was not qualified to make such assessments, it just didn't *look* like a gun that had been fired. Who the fuck had been shooting?

I looked around. Zengatronic was gone.

The door flew open. Jim Kim's dirty little potato head. He looked down at the dying handsome cop.

Then he shot me.

FORGET IT, MARGE, IT'S CHINATOWN

I report the following in good faith, but the years of forgetting have pressed their collective weight on my memory. Many of the truths we thought would ultimately come to light have remained obscured. Jim Kim, good man, did not shoot to kill. I was out of the hospital in a week. Because forensic science had determined I fired no real shots, I was released after thirty or so hours of inconclusive questioning.

In the months immediately following my release from the hospital, I tried to assemble as much information as possible, envisioning a publishable book. Last year, while cleaning out the storage space where my sister and I have kept all my mother's belongings, I came across one of my old elementary school yearbooks. In the page for Ms. Hill's fourth grade class, there is a Tovah Bernstein, but she is listed in the "not pictured" section.

Needless to say, I cannot remember a thing about her.

THE POLICE INVESTIGATED BFG LLC, but found no evidence of anything.

INSPECTOR SIDDHARTHA FINCH survived his wounds, but immediately retired from the force. Last I heard from Kim, who visits from time to time, Finch and his wife, Sarah, had moved to a beach in Indonesia, where she paints and teaches at a local school. He surfs and contributes to the long line of Marxist histories of San Francisco.

Before he left, Inspector Finch asked me to meet with him for one last set of questions. We met at the Java Beach Café on Sloat Avenue, across the street from the city zoo. He had just finished up a surfing session. A healthy satisfaction radiated out of his red, scruffy cheeks. His teeth were an unnerving shade of white. He kept pitching his head forward to let an endless stream of water pour out of his nostrils. After about three of these dumps, he apologized and explained himself. The surf had been large and in charge. The water gets pounded up into your sinuses.

His voice carried a noticeable, almost breezy detachment that seemed incongruous with the seriousness, or, at least, the violence of the events he began to describe. Honestly, I found myself getting a bit annoyed because the separation so clearly came from a genuine sense of superiority to the concerns at hand, the way it might sound to listen to Leontyne Price or Maria Callas breeze through the songbook of Sheryl Crow. At first, I wrote this off to the corrosive effects of constant sunlight and ocean water on the brains of the California surfing male, but after a short period of time it became all too obvious that Siddhartha Finch was, perhaps unwittingly, following the path of his namesake.

I asked him about it. We had been shot together. Part of me was curious to know how he had dealt with the trauma, sure, but more, I was upset to know someone had whipped more out of the experience.

He said yes, shit bothered him less than it had in the past. I asked some specific questions and dropped some holy Eastern names. He just shook his head, steered the conversation back to some other detail.

It was clear he didn't think I'd understand.

When he was done telling me about the catfish and the kidnapping and what had happened to him at the 12 Galaxies, Finch reached into a plastic shopping bag and pulled out a thick slab of printer paper. He said, "This was on a thumb drive found on the person of James Sanders. Thought you'd be interested."

It was *You're My Only Home,* the autobiographical novel I had started while in graduate school, but had never finished. Someone or something had gone ahead and added about 140 pages. A bittersweet, aching ending had been tacked on. I tried to protest, but Finch waved me off. He said he already knew. The book was not entirely my work. And then, having already anticipated the question he knew I wouldn't ask, he said, "Parts of it were good."

I exhaled. He asked me to please read over it. He was going to go catch a second surf session. When I get back, he said, we'll talk more.

I admit: Whoever had finished the novel had done a pretty decent job. The added scenes were lifted, albeit delicately, from other immigrant novels—recently acculturated children practicing their new American signatures, shared pickles, sports-related humiliations, the distance of aunts, the unbearable weight of a father's disappointment. The characters made more sense, meaning they acted more like characters should. I also discovered slight edits to my original text—a word missing here and there, a slight rephrasing of bits of dialogue, a moment of levity added here or there to flesh out a feeling.

When all these credits and erasures were amassed, the effect was, well, pleasant. At least, pleasant enough.

Finch returned, hair dripping, schmucky smile still expanding. He asked what had changed. (Malthus and Herzog were both right. In this overcrowded world, who can still tolerate those pioneering men who lash themselves to the by-products of natural chaos? Surfers, mountain climbers, those who interpret their dog's tolerance of their cat as anything more than a thoroughly humiliated animal's capitulation, why do you so completely deny our misery?)

I pointed out the phantom edits, offered up some feebly pulsing thoughts on what and why, all of which revolved around the idea that somebody was trying to create a more functional killer, an understandable psychopath who couldn't just be explained away with a "Whatever happened to crazy?" Finch, for his part, kept interrupting. Not to ask questions or encourage, but to shit out a stream of yessirs, of courses, and that's what I thoughts.

I realized he had already figured it all out. But when I asked him what exactly was so fucking obvious, he prattled off something about simple minds, complex minds, a fat man, and the Big Friendly Giant. He said if I was really into all that Eastern shit, I should just enjoy the path of figuring it out for myself.

He started stacking up the various cups and plates on our table. As he got up to leave, he slapped me on the shoulder and said, "Congratulations, chief. I don't think they expected you to be you."

I didn't know how to ask him to stay, but there have been times when

I have wondered how the course of my life might have changed if I had been privy to what Finch really meant.

Instead, I have been stuck with my own interpretation. So it goes.

ABOUT FIVE YEARS ago, a novel called *Shards of Madness* was published by one Jeff Kim, a twenty-nine-year-old sous chef turned author from Flushing. The novel was a fictional rendering of the life of Cho Seung-Hui, and although the story stopped short of trying to explain whatever happened to crazy, it carried its deliberately unnamed narrator through a lifetime of humiliations. The less specific parts of the narrative, namely, the father, the mother, the disappointments of his childhood, and the way his Koreanness infected, well, everything, were lifted straight out of the phantom edits to my first novel.

What could I have done with that information?

I didn't finish the book. My sister did, though, and wrote me an e-mail. She said she thought I might have liked it.

ONE LAST DETAIL: Two years ago, the lastest megaconglomerate software company unveiled its newest operating system. At the end of a lineup of awaiting avatars, the BFG sits, kindly, grandfatherly, on his perch, his legs dangling off the edge of the toolbar.

NOW, WHENEVER ELLEN hoists up one of our three children, each one a beautiful thing that I can love, but do not quite yet understand, my mind returns to the Baby Molester and her daily attacks on the promenading stroller moms who walked down our block. Somehow, it feels like an unkind memory, but I've long since stopped feeling guilty over it. Because whenever that foggy reverie ends, my memory spits me right back into that storage closet behind the stage of the 12 Galaxies—I can feel the flattened slugs in my legs and shoulder, I can hear Ellen's gasps, as she, shot through the lungs, chases down whatever breath is left.

But relief, sweet Jesus, floods in quickly, because Ellen will do something, anything, with one of the kids or the mail will come in on time or we will argue over whose turn it is to take out the dog or I will catch her smiling at her computer screen. Whenever one of these moments, seemingly random, stumbles into our lives, I will recall, in full colorful detail, running down the sun-blighted hallway of the hospital on the day they called to tell me she would be released. A shadowy figure emerged out of a doorway with an IV hook hovering over its head. I can remember stumbling over a water cooler and a nurse who told me to slow down. As I apologized, the figure and the IV retreated away down the hall. I recognized the breadth of Ellen's shoulders, the effort she, and only she, put into maintaining posture, despite having been shot through the gut.

Whirling dervish Ellen, best of the bears, heading, as always, straight toward the goal.

I asked the nurse, "Who is that woman?"

ACKNOWLEDGMENTS

This novel would not have been possible without the help of Lindsay Sagnette, Jim Rutman, Rivka Galchen, Francisco Goldman, Kate Steilen, Noelle Daly, Ramesh Pillay, and Casey Koppelson.

ABOUT THE AUTHOR

JAY CASPIAN KANG was born in Seoul and grew up in Boston and North Carolina. He received his BA from Bowdoin and his MFA from Columbia, and has published work in the *New York Times Magazine,* where he is a regular contributor; *Wired; Deadspin;* TheAtlantic.com; and the *Morning News.* Kang is currently an editor for *Grantland,* Bill Simmons's online magazine focusing on sports and pop culture. He lives in Los Angeles.

ABOUT THE TYPE

Touted for their versatility, William Caslon's type families had always enjoyed popularity and were used almost exclusively by Benjamin Franklin. While artistic director of Berthold AG, Günter Gerhard Lange researched Caslon's 1725 types and their seventeenth-century Dutch forerunners to create his revival typeface. Lange released Berthold Caslon Book in 1977. Due to its transitional legibility, Berthold's Caslon is a popular choice for text as well as for display work.